REPRISAL

Joe Daniel

Every effort has been made to obtain the necessary permissions with reference to copyright material, both illustrative and quoted. We apologise for any omissions in this respect and will be pleased to make the appropriate acknowledgements immediately to this novel's e-listing or subsequently in any future editions when this paperback is published or finally also marketed as an audio book.

Cover illustration and general design were created using Amazon Kindle Publishing's guidance and software supported by Microsoft Word.

Imprint: Independently published

An unequivocal 'thank you' once again to my long suffering Editor, Stephen Knight, who has read and re-read the manuscript not only to correct spelling and grammatical errors but also importantly to review the story's flow for readers

Dedication

For all of the Ukrainian civilian and military blood being spilt to defend and ultimately recapture its sovereign land in the name of democracy and freedom for the World

READER'S QUICK REFERENCE LISTING TO THE CHARACTERS NAMES & ROLES IN ORDER OF APPEARANCE

Grzegorz Politczek – Lieutenant-General, Poland's Head of ABW (Poland's Counter-Intelligence Ministry)

Radek Król – Major GROM Polish Special Forces, accredited SEAL, & ABW counter intelligence (designated successor to Colonel Kuba Pawlukowicz within ABW's Special Forces & Counter-Intelligence Department)

Alexandra Król – Radek Król's wife & a former UK SAS Captain in MI6

Tomek & Ewa Król – Radek Król's parents

Ruslan Laskutin – Colonel General, Head of Russian Federation GRU Forces

Igor Yedemsky – Colonel, GRU & Counter-Intelligence

Massoud Ghasemi – Brigadier-General Iranian Revolutionary Guard Aerospace Force

Yaghoub Norouzi – Brigadier-General Iranian Revolutionary Guard Quds Force

Kuba Pawlukowicz Retd – former Colonel ABW Special Forces, & Counter-Intelligence

Witoria Hanko –Colonel, ABW Head of Cyber Security & Geopolitical Counter Intelligence section

Jan Chmura – Colonel, ABW Special Forces, & Counter-Intelligence

Pawel Adamski – Major, ABW, aide-de-camp to Lieutenant-General Politczek

Matt Elliott – Major, former SAS Captain now MI6 officer

Stepan Nalyvaichenko – Colonel Ukrainian Army former Special Forces now Ukrainian Secret Service officer

Timor Morozov – Major-General Russian Army Luhansk Region

Boris Ivanov – Major, GRU & aide-de-camp to Colonel General Laskutin

Tomek Jureki – GROM Team 6

Piotr Vrubel – GROM Team 6

Kuba Michnik – GROM Team 6

Wotjek Tarnowski – GROM Team 6

Pawel Boruch – GROM Team 6

Rafal Dudek – GROM Team 6

Kacper Stodola – Master-Sergeant Polish Navy Seal Special Forces J W Formosa GROM Team 6

Grzegorz Jablonski – Lieutenant Commander of newly formed GROM Team 8

Fedor Romanenko – Kapitan Ukrainian Secret Service Internal Security

Artur Kovtun – Sergeant Ukrainian Secret Service Internal Security
Aleksandr Marchuk – Head of the Ukrainian President's Office
Father Andrii Polischuk – Priest in the Ukrainian Orthodox Church
Irina Shevchenko – secretary in the Ukranian Presidential Secretariat
Dmytro Koval – Kommidor in Naval Intelligence and Head of Security at the underground Government complex in Kyiv
Ramzan Kadyrov – President of Chechnya
General Bolat Abubakarov deceased – former commander of the 1st Chechen Regiment – killed in action March 2022
Vladimir Bogdanov - FSB Director Special Programmes for the President
Kirill Vasilyev - FSB Director Special Programmes for the President
Yevgeny Prigozhin – Russian Leader of the Wagner Mercenary Force
Pawel Nowak – orderly at Jana Pawla II hospital Krakow, FSB sleeper
Musa Usumov – Chechen Intelligence Officer
Valentin Konnikov – freelance assassin for hire
Jean-Paul Moreau – freelance assassin for hire
Peter van de Berg known only as **'the Surgeon'** - freelance assassin & master of disguise namely Professor Lars Andersson; Hans Fischer; Tommaso Genovese; Marcel Durand; & Dieter Müller
Astrid Johansson – administrator in Lund University's Rector's Secretariat
Nikolai Patrushev – former FSB Head & still a member of the Siloviki
Karel Veselý – Prague based armourer to the underworld of crime & assassins
Adek Landa – Senior Inspektor in Poland's Central Bureau of Investigation
Monique Vicot – junior detective in Bouches-du-Rhône Police Prefecture

[**GROM** - the Polish military equivalent of Special Forces units like the United States' Delta force, Green Berets, and SEALS, the United Kingdom's SAS, and Israel's Sajjeret Matkal. **GROM Team 6** – were an elite unit credited with numerous battle honours and led by Major, now Colonel Król. After its historic battles in the Forests of Sumy, the numeric '6' was no longer allocated by Poland's High Command out of respect for the Unit's service and sacrifice]

Table of Contents

Chapter 1

Some weeks had passed since Lieutenant-General Politczek had visited the Król Family compound in Niepolomice. Radek was already undergoing physiotherapy thrice weekly at the new University Hospital in Jakubowskiego on Krakow's eastern periphery. The surgery for his complicated fracture had been a success in ensuring the cartilage network hardened as new blood vessels made new bone. The repaired femur gradually became normal bone leaving the metal splints to be removed shortly before Radek would be passed fit for active duty. Nevertheless, a femur fracture is very painful and full recovery is measured in months not days. Placing any weight on his right leg to stand up or even walk would be very difficult and extremely painful even for a battle hardened Special Forces soldier or indeed any physically fit human being in their late thirties suffering such an injury.

Radek's femur fracture could only be classified as severe. Although the orthopaedic surgeon had ensured in the operation that the straightness and length of his leg had been achieved, it was now the joint responsibility of the physical therapists assigned to his recovery and Radek himself, as the patient, to regain full mobility - the objective being to return in Radek's case to active duty, if not combat deployment, as quickly as humanly possible. This meant teaching Radek how to be mobile using crutches without putting any weight on his right leg until the femur had healed - some two to three months away. In Radek's case, the damage to his left shoulder by another bullet also made initially a wheelchair necessary before graduating to crutches. The head injuries inflicted by shrapnel had been simultaneously removed by the operating surgeons when dealing with his leg and shoulder combat wounds. Apart from the physical therapy sessions at the hospital, a home exercise programme, to complement such out-patient treatment, had become part and parcel of his daily routine. Such an intensive regime was to rebuild leg muscle strength of a fractured leg that had lost more than fifty per cent of that strength within the first week of surgery.

Whilst Alexandra and Ewa Król were like two mothering hens around Radek as their homemade cooking began to replace his lost kilos, there was a distant grimness in his eyes - yet his general demeanour was unchanged. He played with Maya as best he could and took his invalid status in good heart. The St Bernards who would in normal times be jumping all over him and playfully wrestle him to the ground now formed a protective shield around him. These giant dogs simply stood up blocking access to him. Alexandra and Ewa understood, even as close family members, biscuit bribes would be necessary so as to deliver yet another batch of homemade 'golomki' in a spicy tomato sauce to Radek. Notwithstanding the major surgery undertaken to repair & eventually heal his broken body, whether a hero of Poland or not, first and foremost Radek was a human being and even

2

he, considering what had happened, could suffer some form of mental distress. Alexandra and Tomek Król, with their military backgrounds, were aware of the burden that Radek carried as a living hero of Poland – a chest full of medals including twice Poland's highest medal for valour - the Virtuti Militari knights cross. For a quiet and humble man whose leadership qualities had been tested again and again in the service of his country, Radek had faced once more the horror and burden of war in the forests of Sumy and had done extraordinary things in the heat of battle.

Both Alexandra and Tomek could not detect any of the tell-tale symptoms that might indicate Radek could be at risk of suffering Post-Traumatic Stress Disorder (PTSD). Certainly, he did not appear to be feeling upset by things that reminded him of what happened in Sumy or indeed from his tours in Afghanistan and elsewhere. Alexandra knew that her husband slept like a log so there were no nightmares reliving vivid memories, or flashbacks to the past. Radek was looking forward to the birth of their next child around the end of August / early September. He was fully engaged emotionally with the Król family and also enjoying the company of friends round the barbecue as Spring became Summer. His interests in global politics and the progress in prosecuting the war in Ukraine against Russia were unabated. He was just as preoccupied in all the things he used to care about and enjoy. Radek, inspite of being in pain and being weaned off painkillers, was neither irritable nor prone to angry outbursts of frustration, yet there was something deeply hidden and unseen bothering him. Whatever it was that was causing him some inner unease, it was indiscernible to the outside world. Alexandra and Tomek concluded the priority was clearly to help him become fully

3

mobile and once more fit for deployment. Radek would, they knew, in the knowledge of their support, face whatever those demons might or might not be in his own time.

Chapter 2

Colonel Yedemsky was an unhappy man. Why had he been ordered to accompany Colonel-General Laskutin to this rented apartment in Yerevan? His commanding officer had an aide de camp - why was he not fulfilling this baby sitting duty rather than him, a senior GRU intelligence officer? The journey from Moscow had not been direct because of the 'Top Secret' purpose of the meeting in the South Caucasus.

The Armenian capital city's tree lined avenues of coloured stone rise up the hillsides from the Hrazdan river and are framed in the backcloth of those extinct volcanic peaks of Mount Aragats and Mount Azhdaak to the north with Mount Ararat across the Turkish frontier to the south. The choice of Yerevan by both parties was not for atheistic or picturesque reasons for a Spring meeting. For the Iranians, it was more convenient than travelling to Baku in Azerbaijan and their preference. With Russia's historical and current military ties with Armenia, Yerevan was understandably a more comfortable choice for them.

The rented apartment was a few streets away from the large Embassy of the Islamic Republic of Iran in Budaghyan Street. Notwithstanding the flat had been swept for any electronic bugging devices and the remaining apartments were either empty or housing Russian Embassy staff, an Iranian Revolutionary Guards Quds team swept the entire building again and insisted on every apartment being vacated for 2 hours before and after the scheduled meeting with armed Quds personnel stationed in every apartment during that time. Whether Laskutin or Yedemsky considered the Iranians demands overkill or not, the reality was Russia needed to procure Iranian military equipment. The war in Ukraine was being lost on the battlefield and a change in strategy was urgently needed. Military planners were focussing on the winter as being the optimum time to break the Ukrainian populace's will to continue and force their Government to negotiate a peace. However, Russian manufactured cruise and other missiles cost US$1 million or more. Additionally, the scarcity of microchips, because of Western sanctions, made it necessary to find lower cost alternatives to frighten and scare the indigenous population into submission.

Brigadier-Generals Massoud Ghasemi and Yaghoub Norouzi, respectively of the Iranian Revolutionary Guard (IRG) Aerospace and Quds Forces, sat down facing Laskutin and Yedemsky after handshakes as black tea and water were served.

'Gentlemen, we understand that Russia wishes to purchase specific armaments manufactured by the IRG. We need to formalise the quantity of such weapons and price including our capacity to manufacture and supply such quantities'

'General Ghasemi we would like to place an initial order for two thousand four hundred Shahed 136 kamikaze drones for delivery over the next six to twelve months' responded Laskutin.

'We can with some adjustment from our initial strategic stockpile provide a drawdown of some five to six hundred units for delivery in September. However, we will need to manufacture sufficient unmanned aerial vehicles of this model to replenish the drawdown from our strategic reserve and then going forward deliver quarterly from November around four hundred units. Whilst our Supreme Leader, Ali Hosseini Khamenei, has stipulated we must do everything possible to assist you in your efforts to resist the United States' and NATO's war-mongering proxy presently controlling Ukraine, we are also suffering Western sanctions that hinder our ability to manufacture greater numbers.'

'So over the next twelve months, we are talking about a delivery of one thousand eight hundred units General Ghasemi?'

'Correct – a contract in US dollars and a price per Shahed 136 drone of US$20000 has already been discussed with your procurement people. We will organise shipment across the Caspian directly into Russian Territory at which point your Volvograd Military Logistics will, I understand, become involved.'

'Agreed General, but it is my understanding that you will be providing some initial training and instruction to our tactical units.'

'Yes Colonel-General Laskutin we will be sending in late summer training teams dealing with maintenance, spares, and importantly coordinated targeting for swarm attacks. It was a pleasure for Brigadier-General Norouzi and me to meet you.'

Without further ado, the Iranian officers nodded and left the apartment with their special protection unit. Both sides to the negotiation were deliberately not in uniform and within thirty minutes Laskutin and Yedemsky were airborne on a flight that to an external eye looked like a civilian jet charter for two busy businessmen. Sharing a bottle of Zyr vodka as they headed back to Moscow, Yedemsky was ordered by Laskutin to begin compiling a comprehensive list of infrastructure targets city by city and town by town across Ukraine with his military counterparts in the Russian Army's Strategic Planning unit. In Laskutin's words, down to the last sub-station, pump house, factory, residential block, and brick – Ukraine was to become an inhospitable pile of rubble unfit for human habitation, a wasteland. The objective was to create the stench of fear amongst the civilian population from such attrition. A cowed, cold, and desperate Ukrainian people would demand its politicians made peace on any basis. This was the Kremlin's strategy to achieve peace on solely Russia's terms.

Chapter 3

The cherry blossom had disappeared across the Król compound with colour restored temporarily by plum and apple blossom from the other fruit trees. Radek had made good progress by end of June with crutches returned safely to the University Physiotherapy Department. His core body mass had been recovered with the use of supervised weight training. A combination of structured home exercises and specific work by individual trainers in the University's hydrotherapy pool had helped him regain muscular strength to his injured leg. Similarly, his left shoulder no longer ached from that dull and constant pain, similar to muscle fatigue after a strenuous work out, as his damaged tendons had healed. Radek began using a cane as he began walking with the plaster cast removed. Initially just to the compound gate and, as days turned into weeks in high summer, he was soon walking unaided as his body weight was placed on his right leg. It was as if the Ukrainian forces having raised their flag over Snake Island *(the sliver of land in the Black Sea off the coast of Odesa)* and the earlier the sinking of the Moskva *(the flagship of Russia's Black Sea fleet)* had, whilst raising Ukraine's morale, similarly raised Radek's determination to make a full recovery. Clearly, these actions on the battlefield of the Black Sea had eased, if not removed, the threat of a sea-borne invasion of Odesa and also stymied Russia's advance along the coastline, apart from further eroding Moscow's aura of invincible naval power.

The entire Król Family had sat, like many people across the world watching the nightly television news broadcasts, grim faced and in shock as the evidence of the retreating Russian Army's atrocities became starkly clear. Bucha and Borodyanka were the first towns after liberation to reveal the horror of extra judicial executions, torture, and humiliation of the local civilian populaces by Russia's military. Sadly such atrocities would prove to be the modus operandi of the invaders across war torn Ukraine as occupied villages, towns, and cities were reclaimed. Russian artillery shelling and missile attacks had obliterated Mariupol into rubble. A strategy of attrition, leaving only scorched earth behind, unchanged from the Soviet Army's actions in World War II – a military policy of utter destruction.

As Radek had begun to slowly jog round the University Hospital Gym at the beginning of August, Ukraine formally launched a counteroffensive in the Kherson region. The Ukrainian Army was finally deploying a range of US and NATO weapons systems, such as HIMARS, to target Russian military infrastructure. This led to the Russian Military high command's decision to redeploy units from the north east of occupied Ukraine to support its positions in the south east. By the end of the month, in a rapid offensive, the Ukrainian Army retook much of the north-eastern Kharkiv region and in doing so, seized the battlefield initiative.

In late August, the Król family were relaxing together on the Ewa's and Tomek's veranda after a light supper. Alexandra was days away from her expected confinement date in terms of giving birth to Radek's and her second child. Little Maya had fallen asleep on her grandfather's chest as the sun began to set. It was this moment in time that Radek decided to share what had been troubling him since leaving the hospital in April.

'I have felt guilty for surviving the forests of Sumy when too many of my unit did not come home to Poland and their friends and families. Why did I deserve to survive when better men in GROM Team 6 paid the ultimate price in the name of freedom?'

The family said nothing in response though tears had quickly welled up in Alexandra's and Ewa's eyes.

'When I have been on so many missions in Afghanistan and elsewhere when I could so easily have been killed, why given my injuries in the forest did I not end my life there like Bartek and Filip? My job was to protect and lead my team all back safely to Gdansk and I failed. The two other men in my unit who met death that day had also absolute trust in me as their commanding officer. Yet they died and I did not. We were behind enemy lines for over six weeks and I have questioned why I allowed our war to become so very personal with the Chechens? Was Loknya sufficient justification? My memories of this fight are mixed from the camaraderie and laughter to the cries of pain above the gunfire and explosions – I am haunted in my quiet moments by these recollections. That said, like previous missions, time will eventually enable today's rawness to fade. Yet their military service on Poland's behalf will be remembered by all current and future people serving within our Special Forces. I am reconciled and proud that my unit's battle in the forests of Sumy was the way it was. Looking back in hindsight is pointless - the past is past and cannot be changed. That is Life.

Nevertheless, I intend next month, before I take up my new posting in ABW and also after our daughter is safely born, to pay my respects to those men who did not make it home. I will visit the Special Forces Cemetery, meet with the other survivors, and most importantly see my fallen comrades' families. This will be a difficult visit to Gdansk for me emotionally but a necessary one to bring me some much needed closure.'

Chapter 4

Colonel Kuba Pawlukowicz's retirement date was officially September 30th. However, his retirement party at ABW's Rakowiecka Street offices took place on Tuesday the 20th with the Prime Minister, Minister of Defence, and numerous other senior military officials and members of the General Staff in attendance. Kuba had during September started increasingly to meet Radek to ensure a smooth transition of his portfolio and by the middle of the month they were in daily contact whether by encrypted phone or email messages. Thus on Monday September 26th Radek found himself in the Rakowiecka Street building and in Kuba's former office that was now his. He had hardly had a moment to take in his new surroundings and take a sip of his Starbucks takeout coffee before a knock on the open office door announced the unscheduled arrival of Colonel Witoria Hanko.

'Apologies for cornering you before your feet are hardly under the desk but this is urgent.'

Having gestured that she should sit in one of the vacant chairs in front of his desk, Witoria continued.

'Swedish Measuring Stations recorded in the early hours of this morning two strong underwater explosions to the east of the Danish island Bornholm and south of the Swedish mainland in the vicinity of the Nord Stream 1 and 2 gas pipelines. Danish, Swedish and German vessels and helicopters have been dispatched to the incident site and we should then have a better handle on what appears to be a deliberate act of sabotage.'

'Who do you think is responsible?'

'Too early to speculate Radek until we hear more from the Danes, Swedes, and Germans let alone what Gazprom and the Russians have to say. Nevertheless, the old man (Lieutenant-General Grzegorz Politczek) will undoubtedly want all our thoughts later this morning given his regular Monday meeting later this afternoon with the Prime Minister. I am going now similarly to advise Colonel Chmura of this development in the Baltic and I will email you both with updates as I hear from my Danish, Swedish, and German counterparts or others.'

As the morning went on, it transpired that substantial gas leaks of methane bubbling to the surface were visible from some distance with the largest being more than a kilometre in diameter. A subsequent mail from Witoria commented that the Nord Stream sabotage had to be seen in the broader context of the ongoing war in Ukraine and President Putin's determination to succeed. The Russian pseudo-referendums and annexations of the occupied territories were all part of that broader conflict between Russia and the West. The United States, the European Union, and especially an enlarging NATO with Finland's and Sweden's joint decision to apply for membership in May had changed irreparably the geopolitical balance. Thus the gas

13

market had also become a battleground within an emerging energy war as the West sought to reduce to zero reliance on Russian Energy. Was the sabotage of Nord Stream I and II merely a coincidence because the inauguration of Nord Stream II on Tuesday and the gas pipeline due to start operating October 1st timely? Similarly, Gazprom had been substantially reducing supply through Nord Stream I over the summer citing maintenance and turbine replacement as the reasons. Yet the incidents did not appear to threaten the Polish-Danish-Norwegian gas pipeline directly, albeit the explosions did occur alarmingly close to its route in Danish waters.

Later a further mail from Witoria stated that in 2021 both pipelines were inspected by specialists from the Russian Ministry of Defence's Main Directorate of Deep Sea Research (GUGI military unit no. 45707). The soldiers were from the underwater sabotage subunit from the naval base of the Russian Baltic fleet at Baltiysk, Kaliningrad. The GUGI unit's focus is to bug communications cables, install movement sensors, and collect the wreckage of ships, aircraft, and satellites from the seabed. Its engineer divers can work at extreme depths of 3000-6000 metres in miniature submarines. Whilst the sea depth around the area of the explosion is only between 70 to 80 metres and within the diving capabilities of specialised scuba divers, the most likely explanation, and consensus opinion of the Danish German and Swedish Intelligence Services, is the damage to the pipelines was most likely caused by a deliberate Russian act. This thesis is made more plausible by the availability of such specialised underwater equipment for sabotage actions being so readily available in the Baltic for the Russians. What is not clear is whether the explosives were already put in

14

place during construction for a remote detonation at some indeterminate date by a say a submersible divers or if the placements were more recently made. GUGI's participation in the pipeline construction work demonstrates that the Kremlin considers the pipelines to be objects of military importance and are subject to special protection including that they can be destroyed by pre-positioned explosive charges. Damaging its own export infrastructure to the exclusive economic zones of European Union would represent a serious escalation in the wider war. It would also highlight the Kremlin's ability and readiness to attack similar facilities perhaps even the Baltic Pipe belonging to Norway, Denmark, and Poland which Russia classes as so-called 'hostile states' amongst others.

The intercom buzzer on his desk unit flashed breaking his chain of thought. It was Major Adamski telling him to head for Grzegorz's Office for a roundtable meeting on the recent explosions in the Baltic that had clearly terminated Russian gas supplies to Europe worsening the economic situation.

Stood looking out over Warsaw from his 8th Floor vantage point, the General turned to join his senior officers at his conference table.

'Witoria copied me in on her emails so Jan begin'

'General, if it is indeed Russia who sabotaged Nord Stream I and II, it would indicate the Kremlin is not only using its supply of energy resources instrumentally but also is sending a signal about the risk to the security of Europe's critical energy infrastructure. For many months, Russia, through Gazprom, has been deepening the energy crisis and tensions by raising uncertainty and chaos on the energy

15

market. This plan has already included decisions to cut off or significantly reduce gas supplies to a number of European customers including Poland, as well as halting or limiting transport of gas via particular routes. This interpretation has been reinforced by the propaganda message created in the Russian media, which has called the damage to the pipelines as an act of sabotage and a *de facto* terrorist act to be blamed on hostile states. In early summer the United States State Department warned Germany about possibility of attacks on energy infrastructure specifically in the Baltic. More recently, Ukrainian intelligence also suggested the heightened risk of Russia launching cyber-attacks on the critical energy infrastructures of not only Ukraine but also countries supporting Kyiv. If the Kremlin is truly ready to undertake such radical action as attacking its own critical energy infrastructure, it demonstrates its far-reaching determination to use the supply of gas as a political weapon. Moscow is most likely hoping that, by sending a signal about its readiness and ability to carry out such acts, it will increase concern and uncertainty across the European Union populations with winter approaching. The objective is to influence political and military support for Ukraine. In addition, we have to ask ourselves, with oil and gas contracts being implemented with China and India, and Europe looking to diversify away entirely from Russian energy, why not destroy Nord Stream I and II destabilising the market further, especially as prices per cubic foot and barrel can only go upwards?'

'Any further news Witoria?'

'None so far General, it seems with so much methane being released it is too dangerous to establish precisely what took place. From Gazprom's perspective, the damage to both pipelines would provide a legal contractual basis, under a *force majeure* clause, to avoid its contractual obligations to supply gas to its European counterparties. The net effect would be to limit the risk and size of any compensation it might have to pay out. It might also have ironically major insurance cover for loss of revenue and profits with Western Insurers, albeit if it transpires the Russian State, which owns Gazprom, is involved I do not see damages for breach of contract being avoided or insurance claims being met.'

'Welcome aboard Radek – your thoughts?'

'General, it is difficult to identify who the potential alternative perpetrators might be. Accusations against the United States, for example, have mainly been coming from traditionally pro-Russian circles. The damage to the pipelines does not change the actual situation with regard to the supply of Russian gas to Europe. Nord Stream II has never been put into operation and transmission through Nord Stream I had already been completely halted. The damage also makes it possible for Russia to use the option of resuming its gas exports instrumentally in its relationships with individual European countries. Dividing the European Union and achieve the easing of sanctions and reducing military and political support for Ukraine is, I agree with Jan, the Kremlin's key objective in weaponising the supply of gas. We do not believe in 'coincidence' in our intelligence world and especially as far as matters Russian are concerned. Only state actors would be capable of sabotaging undersea infrastructure due to the complex nature of the operation making Russia the potential perpetrator. The likes of a Greta Thunberg activist or similar masterminding such a mission does simply not stand close scrutiny. Again I concur with Jan, amongst Moscow's assorted motives, demonstrating its ability to attack critical energy infrastructure will only intimidate the West. The possibility of similar operations against other transmission networks cannot be discounted in particular the gas pipelines in the North Sea. It provides another distraction and worry for European Governments, even if the Kremlin has no intentions of invoking by its actions NATO's Article 4 or 5 *(*for reference, Article 4 means any member state can convene a meeting of NATO members to 'consult' when it feels its independence or security are threatened. In practice, Article 4 has rarely been used but it does send a strong political message globally that NATO is concerned about a particular situation. On the other hand, Article 5 is known as the 'one-for-all and all-for-one' article and is the keystone of NATO as an organization - an 'armed attack' against one member is an attack against all and sets in motion the possibility of collective self-defence. That said, it only commits members to 'assist the party or parties so attacked' and to take 'such action as it deems necessary, including the use of armed force'. It does not automatically result in military action).* Finally, the answer is who has the most to gain from such an attack of sabotage? With that in mind, there is no other suspect but the Kremlin. Perhaps the Danes and Swedes will over the coming months find evidence in the crime scene that will confirm Russian involvement beyond any reasonable doubt. However for now, we must wait even though all the European Union countries' intelligence agencies have reached the same conclusion and strong suspicion of solely Russian involvement.'

'Many thanks, whilst Pawel Adamski is putting a summary of our discussion together for my meeting this afternoon are there any other issues we should be considering?'

'The influx of Ukrainian refugees has given us and our European neighbours a number of issues. Out of the 7.4 million to date crossing European Union borders some 3.2 million including 1.3 million documented labour migrants are here in Poland. Putting to one side the vaccination issue for COVID with less than 50% having at least one dose, the World Health Authority has forecast a potential flu epidemic this winter together with COVID mutations from Omicron to Kraken variants. Whilst such risks fall to the Ministry of Health to mitigate, our remit is to serve and protect. In my opinion General this matter should be front and centre at your meeting this afternoon. I am also concerned that in addition to the limited number of Russian sympathisers in our population, the Ukrainian refugees and labour migrants have merely heightened the security risks for our population – the enemy within.'

'That easy to say Jan but how do you propose the Government addresses such issues?'

'General we should insist at our borders on not only passports being presented by returning Ukrainian citizens but also Polish identification cards. The frequency of such trips and length will flag to both the Ukrainian Security Services and us the need to investigate. There are an increasing number of private vehicles with Ukrainian plates from new mercedes to old wrecks. I would like to see our Police stopping such vehicles and checking the paperwork including passports etc. Again this information will be centralised and cross referenced with our border records for anomalies. Any undocumented refugee will have three months to obtain an identification card. With regard to Ukrainians returning from elsewhere in the Schengen Area, their relevant host country identification cards will be necessary with the information logged on our server. As for COVID variants and Influenza, I will leave that to the Ministry of Health.'

'Ok Jan I will raise both matters under 'Any Other Business. Witoria'

'General, you may recall a Captain, now Major Matt Elliott of the UK's Special Forces and now permanently an MI6 Officer who with Radek successfully exposed amongst other things the Russian spy network in Poland.'

General Politczek nodded - Witoria continued

'... apparently, GCHQ Cheltenham has picked up communications that could indicate a major attack on Russian infrastructure. The 'chatter' is more probably emanating from actual Russian Nationals rather than solely Russian speakers from elsewhere not the Ukrainian Security Services or Military. Ukrainian senior political officials and its high command have repeatedly declared their ultimate intention to destroy the Crimean Bridge as a legitimate military target. However, as the Ukrainian Military have both cruise missiles and drones bringing the Bridge well within their target ranges, 'chatter' hinting at a circuitous land based route rather ruled out the Ukrainians as far as Major Elliott and I were concerned. In fact, even on such slim information the target is seemingly the Crimean Bridge and thus the involvement of dissident Russian groups. Perhaps the real question is what will be the Russia's retaliatory response to a major attack on the Crimean Bridge or any other infrastructure within its perceived territorial borders?'

'Radek?'

'Kuba had become interested lately in Ukraine's efforts to build a secret army of patriots within its occupied territories. This resistance movement will range from being information gatherers to providing detailed coordinates of logistic depots to simply being agent provocateurs disrupting communications to even actual assassinations. In addition, Ukraine's Special Forces were, he believed, beginning to seek high profile targets within Russia. With this in mind, a meeting had already been arranged to meet with Colonel Stepan Nalyvaichenko of the Ukrainian Secret Service in Kyiv. I know Stepan. We worked with him when Team 6 was patrolling the forests and national park of Pripiat Stokid in the last months of 2021. I would like to follow up on Kuba's initiative.'

'Agreed but I am not sure how well Alexandra is going to take the news so soon after giving birth to your second daughter, Marysia, that you are already away to Kyiv!'

Chapter 5

Radek left Niepolomice in the late evening of Friday October 7th in a chauffeur driven Military Mercedes s500. He was met at the Ukrainian Border by Polish Military Police who directed him to one of the armaments convoys heading to Kyiv by rail. Radek was guided by two Ukrainian Military Police soldiers through a dining car where a group of Ukrainian logistic officers and soldiers were already gathered to the adjoining passenger coach. Having stowed his kitbag and dress uniform, he hunkered down to sleep.

Shortly after 05:15 hours, he was awakened to the sound of cheering from the dining car and loud hoots of joy. The celebration was the result of the incumbents receiving the breaking news that at 04:07 CET a large explosion had occurred on the Crimean Bridge. Early reports indicated motorway sections of the bridge had partially collapsed and fuel tanks on the upper rail tracks were ablaze. It would seem Matt's and Weronika's speculative guess was correct. Slipping back slowly into a deep sleep, his mind recalled the nineteen kilometre bridge is the longest in Europe spanning the Kerch Strait between Russia and occupied Crimea. It had been previously the only direct road and rail link. However, the fall of Mariupol in May to the Russian Army had finally enabled a land corridor along the Azoz Sea's western coastline to be established. The bridge is seen as very much President Putin's personal project apart from now being a vital supply link for the Russian war effort in Southern Ukraine. As he toyed with these facts, the Kerch Strait Bridge symbolised the political propaganda of the connection with Crimea and also projected Russian power – what will Putin's response be Radek pondered drifting back into sleep?

Around mid-morning Radek with other passengers unconnected to the logistics rail convoy were disembarked at Pidhirsti Railway Station in the rural south of the Kyiv Metropolis. Colonel Stepan Nalyvaichenko's wide grin was waiting to greet him on what was otherwise desolate platform. As he hugged Radek in a bear like grip with laughter coming from his throat, Stepan welcomed in his words 'the Hero of the Sumy Forests'. Somewhat embarrassed by Stepan's accolade as he momentarily recalled again his lost comrades, he followed the Colonel to the waiting limousine.

'Have you heard the news Radek?'

'You mean about the Crimea Bridge?'

'Yes – who do you believe carried out the attack?'

'Are you trying to tell me that it was not orchestrated by the Ukrainian Secret Service and Military High Command Stepan?'

'Radek – I am asking your opinion.'

'Are you adopting the United States style of response in that you are seeking to neither confirm nor deny any Ukrainian involvement in the attack? Ukraine's Military, whether Special Forces or yourselves in the Secret Service, must logically be the prime suspect. The Russians will not believe or think otherwise let alone the wider world!'

'Calm down Radek. Ukraine has adopted a policy of not immediately claiming responsibility for any attack, especially on Russian soil as opposed to the occupied territories. This is primarily to protect the escape of those individuals whether military personnel or partisans whilst in enemy controlled territory. Such actions are designed to bring home the reality of war directly to the Russian people.

Take the April 1st helicopter attack on the Belgorod fuel depot, our pilots showed extraordinary skills and bravery not only flying barely metres above the tree line and telegraph poles but also doing so at night. Low-flying helicopters are, as you know, still highly vulnerable to short-range air defence systems. Whilst flying at night lessened that risk, it heightened the danger of hitting an object near the ground. This attack alone did not dramatically alter the war but gave a huge boost to the morale of Ukraine's military. At the end of the month, we formally acknowledged the attack.

Similarly, the Crimean August 9th strikes were part of a deliberate response to Russian propaganda efforts to try and distance its own civilians from the conflict. For example, the Saky airbase is near Novofedorivka on Crimea's western coast is a beach area popular with Russian tourists. You only had to see the long queues of traffic as Russian holidaymakers fled all of Crimea to realise how such explosions had undermined Russia's overall military confidence and sense of impunity since 2014. Word of mouth by returning Russians will say far more than State TV about Putin's War of Choice.'

'So Stepan answer the question - was it the home team attacking the Kerch Strait bridge?'

'Although I cannot be a 100% sure, I do not believe this attack was launched by our Military or partisans or embedded patriots or indeed anyone else who is a Ukrainian sympathiser. For me it has the hallmarks of a Russian false flag operation as cover for some impending battle strategy. Frankly just how can a truck loaded with explosives suddenly appear travelling towards Simferopol and also have been allowed to pass through an entry checkpoint onto the bridge beggars belief? It has to mean the paperwork of the driver and vehicle checks passed muster. So was this a regular armament delivery of high explosive that mysteriously and accidentally exploded or was the detonation made remotely by the FSB or GRU as an integral part of a false flag operation? Whilst the Russian handling of munitions is often careless and haphazard resulting in dangerous explosions, the early provision of camera footage indicates the start of a propaganda exercise to my mind. This news has put to the back page our coordinated attack last night on a cargo train in Ilovaisk by partisans within the occupied Donetsk region. Similarly, the last power line connecting the Zaporizhzhia nuclear plant to Ukraine's electrical power grid was damaged and disconnected today due to shelling from Russian forces. What also makes me know that this is a false flag operation is that for some months we have had the capability to destroy the entire bridge either with cruise missiles or Turkish supplied drones or both yet our High Command has not issued such an order. In addition, my instructions from High Command have been to ensure locally based Crimean patriots leave the bridge well alone. The strategic reasoning is to leave an exit route back into Mother Russia for its retreating army as we retake all the occupied territories from 2014. At that point, as the last Russian boot leaves our country's soil, the Crimea Bridge will then be no more.'

'Stepan, I believe your assessment is a well-thought through analysis. I do worry though what the Kremlin is hatching under the cover of such a false flag diversion in the light of your Army's continuing successes on the battlefield.'

The military limousine came to a halt outside a non-descript eight storey building adjoining the Government's Building in Hrushevsky Street. Stepan led Radek through security to the lifts as they descended six floors.

'Radek you have twenty minutes to shower shave and change into your dress uniform. You do not want to keep my President waiting!' Radek disappeared into the adjoining bathroom to Stepan's office without any further urging.

'My God Radek is there any room on your chest for any more metal?' Radek's face merely recorded a somewhat embarrassed and sheepish grin. Walking through a warren of corridors and blast protection doors, Stepan entered the relevant passcode for entry, codes that changed constantly for the Government's security. As they wove their way eight floors below ground towards the President's Office housed within the Government's deep bunker, Stepan and Radek were also stopped a few times to check their identification and also to confirm the appointment with the President. After what seemed a long time of scurrying about in subterranean tunnels, an armed escort showed them into the Cabinet's Conference Room and then withdrew.

President Zelensky surrounded by his personal retinue and protection team entered. A smartly dressed soldier amongst a sea of battlefield fatigues, especially at 188cms tall, wearing the distinctive four cornered cap (rogatywka) of the Polish Military with a red and silver cap band (signifying the intelligence and special forces arms of Poland's military) rather stood out. Radek came to attention clicking his dress cavalry boots as he saluted.

President Zelensky smiled 'The Hero of the Sumy Forests does not need to stand to attention in my presence or anyone's. Please stand easy.'

Radek lowered his saluting right hand but remained at attention out of respect for the man who symbolised Ukrainian resistance to Putin's malevolent Russia.

'Ukraine owes Poland's GROM Team 6 an enormous debt of gratitude for its fight against those Chechen murderers and rapists in the forests of Sumy after the brutality of Loknya. For those acts alone, it is my honour on behalf of the people of Ukraine to present you with the Order of the Gold Star – our highest military award for valour. At a personal level, your Team's actions in the Pripiat Stokid National Park also prevented a serious assassination attempt on my own life and that of my close family. Your

27

President has told me Colonel of the very high regard in which you are held not only in military circles but also by the Polish Government and Poland. It pleases me to see you have recovered from your wounds protecting Ukraine. Again I thank on behalf of Ukraine and myself for being a true friend in our hour of need.'

One of the President's aides handed him the medal to pin on his chest and then the citation scroll.

'Colonel Król enjoy the military dinner organised in your honour tonight.' The President at the urging of his bodyguards turned to leave as Radek saluted. Time was always at a premium for any wartime leader and President Volodymyr Zelensky had proved beyond doubt – cometh the hour cometh the man.

Chapter 6

With the dinner over and the dignitaries including the Polish Ambassador having left, Stepan and Radek were enjoying yet another Remy Martin brandy at the Radisson bar when they were interrupted by the incessant ringing of Stepan's mobile. In the end he reluctantly answered the phone as the scream of air raid sirens began swiftly followed by explosions across Kyiv. Russia's response to their false flag attack on the Crimea Bridge had begun.

Russian forces were now in the process of launching a massive missile and drone attack across all of Ukraine. It would subsequently transpire that the Kremlin envisaged such attacks would continue for months throughout the entire winter. Previous attacks, that had hit residential and other non-military buildings from hospitals to kindergartens had, for a few commentators, been excused in part as basic inaccurate targeting together with an in-built technology failure of Russian missiles. What now became clear over the coming days was a clear strategic change in the Kremlin's pursuit of its war aims against Ukraine given its battlefield failures. Airstrikes and shelling were now specifically hitting critical infrastructure and civilian buildings in cities like Kyiv, Kharkiv, Lviv, Dnipro, Odesa, and Zaporozhye killing many non-combatant civilians including children. The strikes would destroy in a matter of days 30% of all Ukrainian power stations causing power outages across the entire country. The Russian game plan was to make Ukraine's civilian population face the oncoming winter without electricity and ultimately heating in blackouts; coercion to break the will of the Ukrainian populace to resist and support the Government in the fight against the Russian aggression. Tactics of annihilation of the country's infrastructure and wanton destruction of property to rubble, let alone the loss of innocent civilian life, merely reinforced Russia's ultimate goal to destroy Ukraine as an independent State.

Stepan led the way back to the Hrushevsky Street building through the darkness and then into the War Room. As they drank mugs of steaming black coffee, Colonel Nalyvaichenko began to answer Radek's earlier questions

'Since February 24th, we have begun to copy the British Special Operations Executive (SOE) World War II organisation in terms of forming a secret army in the occupied territories and in the borderlands of Russia together with Belarus. The prime role of such patriots is currently reconnaissance for the targeting of our missiles to destroy military logistics sites from munitions to fuel dumps. We are moving towards sabotage behind enemy lines utilising a combination of trained partisans and our own Special Forces. However, whilst militarily we are far better prepared than in 2014, our Secret Service has to face the harsh fact that from Soviet times, Russia has had an in-built group of sympathisers established over many decades as 'sleepers'. Like my colleagues, I am also very concerned at not only the accuracy but also the use of kamikaze drones attacking our electrical infrastructure down to even substations. Such targeting merely confirms the presence of Russian 'sleepers'. As for the drones, these are not manufactured in Russia but Iran. Recent drone attacks have emanated from the occupied territories and strike me as operators familiarising themselves with the technology. Our air defences are inadequate and under strain. Even if the United States and NATO supply high technology air defence systems tomorrow, we are months away from their deployment as training Ukrainian personnel will take time. In the interim, we can foresee the Russians using, in addition to cruise missiles, swarms of drones that will simply overrun our air defence. Dark and cold days will become even darker with daily power cuts for extended periods. Much of our electrical power grid stems from Soviet times. This means that parts have long since stopped being manufactured making repairs even more difficult.'

The teleprinter began to spring into life and Stepan walked to the machine. Tearing the paper along the perforation, he handed the text to Radek. It read...

Alexander Bastrykin - Russian Chief Investigator reports, at 06:07 Moscow Time (04:07 CET) October 9th, the explosion on the Crimea Bridge was set off by a truck on the motorway part of the Kerch Strait. This led to a fire engulfing seven fuel tanks of a train that was en route to the peninsula as two motorway sections of the bridge partially collapsed. The explosives were loaded at Odesa at the beginning of August and shipped through Bulgaria, Armenia and Georgia into Russia. On October 7th, these explosives were loaded onto a Russian truck bound for Simferopol, albeit the Federal Security Service (FSB) believe more than one truck had been used in Russia to transport the bomb. The 22,770 kgs of explosives were transported on 22 pallets. In connection with this terrorist act, the FSB have detained eight people, five Russians and three other people believed to be Ukrainian citizens. The FSB in a separate incident detained an Ukranian male believed to be involved in planning another bombing in Bryansk. According to the FSB, this individual is cooperating with the investigation. Message Ends

'The speed at which this statement was released including the precise amount of explosive coupled with the apparent efficiency of the FSB immediately having suspects in custody rather proves your argument about a false flag operation Stepan.'

'Cold comfort Radek! We are about to see drones deployed on a scale never seen before across my country carrying out infrastructure strikes.

Chapter 7

Major-General Timor Morozov had been recalled from the Luhansk front to Moscow and found himself sitting in an ante-room outside Colonel-General Laskutin's Grizodubovoy Street office. It was unnerving to be ordered to leave immediately his post especially when President Putin was replacing the general staff. The 'Special Military Operation' had to date been a failure as far as the Russian Army was concerned. Did this mean retirement or even worse a posting to Severomorsk in the Arctic? His wife enjoyed living in St Petersburg with their children settled in local schools. A Severomorsk posting would mean divorce. As he was speculating about his military and domestic future, the door to the Colonel General's office was opened by Major Ivanov, his aide de camp.

'The Colonel-General will see you now.'

Morozov stood up, put on his General's cap, and walked through the open door nodding to Ivanov. Standing to attention, clicking his boot heels together simultaneously saluting, he was in front of Colonel-General Laskutin who was sat behind his desk. Waving him to sit in one of the vacant chairs, Ruslan Laskutin spoke.

'Ivan I would like you to tell me about the battle for control of the Sumy forests in March and April this year.'

'The Chechen 1st Regiment was initially deployed on the fringes of the forests and along the frontline. However High Command decided to utilise some of Kadyrov's battle hardened Chechens to root out any Ukrainians operating behind our forward lines. The commencement of the campaign began badly. A company of Chechens was eliminated completely after it had destroyed a small hamlet, Loknya. General Bolat Abubakarov, their commanding officer, went to the village the following day to establish why the unit had failed to report. He was killed by a single shot to the head. In my view, Abubakarov was coldly assassinated. The result was the Regiment declared a blood feud *(chir)* on whosoever or whatever Ukrainian outfit was operating across and within the forests. Out of 900 Chechen fighters, after less than 4 weeks, only 166 were still capable of active service as we withdrew to our Belgorod base with just 51 wounded. The rest were dead or had died from their wounds. Instead of striking fear into our enemy's mind and that of its civilian population, Ukraine's Special Forces had seemingly delivered a hammer blow to our morale let alone removed the effectiveness of the Chechen 1st Regiment as a fighting unit.'

Laskutin hit one of the buttons on his desktop intercom – 'Colonel, can you please join me in my office.'

Moments later, Colonel Yedemsky entered and sat in the remaining vacant chair in front of the Colonel-General's desk.

'Oleg what do we know about who was deployed in the forests of the Sumy during March and April.'

'GRU do not believe Ukrainian Special Forces were deployed behind our lines in the Sumy Forests. Whilst Poland will deny the fact, we are increasingly certain that a Polish GROM unit was involved. Our reasoning was initially battlefield chatter after the relief of Sumy and the withdrawal of our forces. Then our locally based sources highlighted the return of wounded soldiers to the Polish border. A hospital orderly working in Krakow's Jana Pawla II hospital confirmed a badly wounded Polish Officer had been helicoptered in from the border. Major Radek Król was that officer that can only mean GROM Team 6 were the unit operating in the Sumy Forests. Subsequently, the formal funeral in Gdansk for the dead of GROM Team 6 and the attendees as far as GRU is concerned put their involvement beyond doubt.'

'Ramzan Kadyrov has spoken personally to President Putin regarding the losses suffered by the Chechen 1st Regiment. Kadyrov has asked for our intelligence on who was involved and our assistance in locating them. This is about revenge being exacted by Chechen assassins wherever the surviving individuals are. Oleg your thoughts?'

'Colonel-General, my concerns are that providing photographs and locational details will, with Chechens exacting a caucus style blood feud, mean close family also being executed brutally. In addition, there is an unspoken agreement that the United States, NATO, or other West leaning states will not assassinate our senior people and similarly us theirs. It is of course different if 'enemy'

35

personnel are operating in one's country but neither side want to open this particular Pandora's Box. There is a clear difference as far as State Policy is concerned in that Russian Nationals, traitors to Russia, cannot escape retribution by hiding in a Western country.

Radek Król is well known to GRU as a respected adversary. Recently promoted to Colonel on the retirement of Colonel Kuba Pawlukowicz at ABW, his assassination by Chechens or indeed anyone else on Polish Territory would provoke a massive reaction. Król has just been awarded Ukraine's Order of the Gold Star to add his many citations for bravery and valour in action, including Poland's highest honour twice. In my view, GRU should not involve itself in Kadyrov's thirst for revenge or help in any way to identify the survivors of GROM Team 6. If anything, we should use our back channels to alert Poland to this threat.'

An uneasy silence filled the room as Laskutin and Morozov considered the gravity of Colonel Yedemsky's words.

'General, you are to return to Belgorod immediately. As far as you are concerned, this meeting never took place and what you have heard today from Colonel Yedemsky is to be instantly forgotten – that is an order.' Morozov stood, replaced his General's cap, saluted and left.

With the door closed, Laskutin turned to Yedemsky and spoke.

'Your analysis is correct Oleg. Kadyrov's thugs are nothing less than barbaric animals and whatever took place in Loknya signed for many of them their death warrant. Whilst our High Command's, or rather our President's strategy is to intimidate and terrorise the civilian population by indiscriminate bombing and shelling, we cannot enable Kadyrov's murderous assassins free rein in Poland or elsewhere.'

'How will we deal with the President's request Colonel-General?'

'You must delete all information and records pertaining to the Sumy Forests Oleg. Key informers and witnesses are to be removed and posted to one of our GRU stations in Siberia. Nothing must be left to chance as the President will ask the FSB to investigate - that will include access to our files and servers. GRU's response will be that our records indicate that unknown Ukrainian partisans were probably responsible rather than regular forces.'

'Understood.'

Chapter 8

Lieutenant-General Politczek removed the SIM from the burner phone breaking it into small pieces before discarding them into a shredder. As for the phone, a few successive thumps of his boot heel had the casing and drive destroyed. Leaning over to his desk intercom and pushing his aide's designated button, Major Adamski was simply requested to ask the Colonels, Chmura and Król, to join him in 'the Chamber'. Whilst known within ABW as 'the Tent', this is a special secure room within a room to prevent electronic eavesdropping for highly sensitive communication. Emanations from internal circuitry can be read remotely as well for LED flat screens, terminals, laptops, keyboards and mobiles hence the Tent is a highly engineered sealed glass box raised off the floor with no electronic kit inside or within the immediate vicinity. Air-conditioning, power, cable adaptors, and filters to prevent signal leakage while allowing in / out communications had been installed together with entry through an airlock.

Jan and Radek joined a grim faced Grzegorz Politczek.

'An un-named source within GRU has used a back-channel to forewarn us of potential assassination attempts in the coming months in Poland of Polish citizens.'

'Do we have any idea who the perpetrators might be?'

'Yes Jan – the survivors of the Chechen 1st Regiment, and probably the brothers, fathers, sisters, and uncles of the 683 killed in the forests of Sumy by Radek's GROM Team 6.'

'Not many then!' sarcastically uttered Jan.

'Presumably General, the targets are the survivors of GROM Team 6 and their close family?'

'Yes Radek I believe so. Ramzan Kadyrov's Chechen fighters are an undisciplined band of murderous thugs as you know from what occurred in Loknya.'

'General what do you believe is the reason for this back-channel being opened?'

'Well I do not think it was because the GRU has suddenly gained a conscience. It has to do with Poland's reaction in particular should such brutal murders take place here. It would open the gates for military, even political, assassination on Russian soil. That is why agents operating in-country can be killed dependent on the circumstances or face incarceration. The purpose of the contact is twofold – one it is not us & two we have provided no intelligence to assist Kadyrov whatsoever.'

'General, I only attended the medal ceremony in Kyiv just a week ago under tight security and hidden from the public gaze or any announcement of any kind. Hence how has the GRU obtained knowledge of the award or that my visit had even taken place?'

'It must mean, within Zelensky's entourage, Government Ministers, staff, and administration operating across the entire bunker, there is a Russian spy who is deeply embedded' said Jan.

'Gentleman, let's park just for a moment this apparent security breach that will be a serious matter for Ukraine's Secret Service. We must concentrate on how we are going to protect the survivors of GROM Team 6 and their families.'

'Yes General' responded the Colonels as one.

'Radek the survivors are your men so outline for us the extent of the problem we now face.'

'Accepting the intelligence is solid, there is no indication as to how quickly or slowly Kadyrov or his team will identify GROM Team 6 as the unit responsible for decimating the 1st Chechen Regiment. Will it be a month, a year, or even longer? Similarly, mounting numerous missions will in turn take time and money – Chechnya is some 2500 to 3000 kilometres away. I am not attempting to dismiss or diminish the seriousness of the threat. Rather it is the length of the fuse for a rural and poorly educated country where North Caucasus tribal blood feuds have been a way of life for centuries. Time is generational for the delivery of that revenge.

The GROM Team that entered the Sumy Forests was an amalgam of Team 6 and 5 under the banner of Team 6 as I was the Senior Officer. We were 16 special forces soldiers in total but only 12 of us survived. Master-Sergeant Kacper Stodola, Tomek Jureki, Piotr Vrubel, Kuba Michnik, Wotjek Tarnowski, and Pawel Boruch are all married men with young families. Some still live on the Gdansk Military and Naval base but not those who have apartments or houses elsewhere in the Tri-City Region. Rafal Dudek sadly died in a motorbike accident with his then girlfriend while holidaying in France this summer. The remaining 4 survivors of GROM Team 6, excluding myself, were bachelors and as far as I know used to live on the Gdansk base. So 10 of the former GROM Team 6, having been passed fit for combat, have been probably been deployed across the remaining GROM units or even possibly a new Team led by a new Officer. However, whether they are currently deployed here or overseas at this moment I do not know.'

'The good news General, and Radek, is the Team 6 survivors have recently been formed into a new unit known as GROM Team 8 under Lieutenant-Commander Grzegorz Jablonski. This decision was understandably taken so as not to ignore or waste the strong bonds of camaraderie amongst these men and fighting spirit clearly present. This is for us a stroke of luck in how we plan Team 8's protection against this ominous threat from Chechnya.'

Lieutenant-General Politczek pushed Major Adamski's button on his intercom –

'Please Pawel find out urgently where GROM Team 8 is presently stationed and its planned deployment orders for the next 6 months. The Colonels and I are waiting.'

'Whilst we wait for details on GROM Team 8, what options come to mind gentlemen?

'If GROM Team 8 was an individual and a civilian, I would be considering witness protection. However, that option is not, in my view, available to us, even if all six families were prepared to consider breaking all ties with relatives and Poland.'

'Jan, I agree. Knowing these men, especially the married ones, there will be fierce resistance to any overseas posting or similar training exercise unless we can confidently provide as good, if not better, protection on the basis they were guarding personally their nearest and dearest.'

'This raises the question seriously gentlemen as to whether GROM Team 8 should even be told about this classified intelligence. Poland is a democracy. We cannot place families and children in a secure compound – it would be no different to them being in a prison. They need the freedom to live their lives and have the inalienable right to do so. With this in mind, I do not consider our soldiers should be made aware, at this moment, of this nebulous albeit real threat from Chechnya. What we have to do now is use all resources of our allies and ourselves to listen and watch for Kadyrov's enquiries to evolve into a real threat with specific Chechens identified. At that point we can eliminate the individuals.'

'General, it is my belief GROM Team 6's covert missions assisting Ukraine over the last 12 months will have inevitably led some local knowledge of who these soldiers were. However, like in life, it will only be the officer leading the combatants who will be remembered by name. This makes Radek a prime target and one that the Chechens will accept as sufficient retribution as they establish his status within Poland.'

'Radek, is Jan correct that even a moderate investigation by your potential assassins in Sumy will flag your name?'

'Sadly General I think Jan is right – I will eventually be the target!'

The General's intercom buzzed and he put Major Adamski on loudspeaker.

'General - GROM Team 8 is on exercise with Finnish Special Forces within the Arctic Circle. They are not expected to report back to Gdansk Headquarters and barracks until the beginning of November. In the New Year, Team 8 is scheduled to be part of a NATO military exercise in Estonia though the precise details are not expected to be announced until its return.'

'Thank you Pawel. Radek you are entitled like Jan and me to a personal protection team. I do not want to hear anymore resistance from you as to why such personnel are necessary.'

'General.' Radek acknowledged the new status quo.

'Jan you are accountable and responsible for mounting a priority intelligence programme. Utilise all available listening posts including the UK's GCHQ and other similar organisations to listen and watch for any red flags as to Kadyrov moving from talk to action. In addition, as part of the information gathering, see whether Georgia's Secret Service with its eyes and ears already in Chechnya can assist us. Radek, with your protection team and no doubt Alexandra plus your father given his Special Forces experience, look with fresh eyes on your domestic security and the safety of the homes in the family compound. Jan you are to have oversight of what is both proposed and actioned in the coming weeks.

For the moment, this classified intelligence remains within ABW. Please also consider how our movements and those of Government Ministers to this building impact our present level of security.'

Chapter 9

Stepan listened intently to Radek's call on a protected and encrypted phone line. The news of Russia's FSB or GRU having a spy at the very heart of Ukraine's Government, let alone within the President's inner circle, was more than an unwelcome surprise.

Ukrainian Security Services had since the commencement of the war detained and launched hundreds of Court cases against informants and collaborators. Many of these people had supported Russia in fighting against Ukraine from even before February 24th as far back as before 2014. With onset of Shahed drone swarms and incoming missiles from Russia increasingly destroying Ukraine's energy infrastructure, Kyiv was again suffering a power blackout. It was self-evident to Stepan, as generators cut-in restoring lighting to his subterranean office, that there were still numerous Russian sympathisers lost in the wider populace still providing precise coordinates for the enemy's targeting. However the immediate problem facing him was now to identify this new and present threat to the Nation's security - a Russian sympathiser or agent operating within the President's inner circle with access to the highest reaches of Government.

Stepan walked the short distance along the corridor to the office where his team, Kapitan Fedor Romanenko and Sergeant Artur Kovtun, were based. Maintaining internal security across the Government offices housed in the interlinking bunkers of central Kyiv was and is a constant and separate war for the Secret Service. Raising human awareness and removing complacency were the never ending daily battles. His unit's focus and particular responsibility was to build a partisan secret army in the occupied territories including also Belarussian and Russian nationals in the border hinterlands opposed to Putin's War of Choice. Nevertheless, for now Stepan and his team were best placed to begin the hunt for the enemy within.

A comprehensive list of the President's retinue and then a second listing all those present when Radek was awarded 'the Order of the Gold Star' some eight days earlier was the starting point of their investigation. The major problem for counter-espionage is age, background, gender, and status are no guide to finding such collaborators. Russian agents were still everywhere in spite of the actions taken by the Ukrainian Security Services. The acronym MICE was the mnemonic device used in counterintelligence to find the motivations that could lead someone to commit treason by becoming an insider threat and collaborating with a hostile agency such as the FSB or GRU. It stands for Money, Ideology, Compromise, and Ego. As Stepan and his team cross-referenced the names including those in the President's secretariat controlling his diary, they knew that out of the thousand or more collaborators already exposed since the invasion - sadly forty seven per cent were politicians and appallingly twenty seven per cent were judges. A dire indictment of a corrupt and rotten system where long overdue reforms only really happened after February 24th such as finally prohibiting Pro-Russian parties. Russian influence had remained, not surprisingly, deeply ingrained in many Ukrainian institutions after nearly 70 years as part of the Soviet Union until of course the seismic shocks of the 2013-14 Maidan Revolution and even more so since Russia's invasions in 2014 and 2022.

Stepan, Fedor, and Artur quickly took off the table the Minister of Interior, his Deputy, and the Deputy Minister of Defence. This left the President's Bodyguards to be reviewed utilising Secret Service records and recent positive vetting reports. The President's Private Secretary was a young widow with two children. Her late husband was a Ukrainian Army Kapitan who had been killed during the defence of Kyiv in March. Whilst on the face of it an unlikely Russian collaborator, Artur still proceeded, like the others, to utilise his computer and internet skills as a 'white hat' from emails to phone records to the dark web to be absolutely certain. Nevertheless finding this Russian Spy required diligent and patient investigative work. Stepan discounted for now anyone who saw Radek arriving at Pidhirsti Railway Station and just might have recognised him by pure chance in his unmarked battlefield fatigues. No one there could have possibly known about his forthcoming award ceremony with the President behind closed doors. They all looked at video recordings of Radek's arrival at the Government complex including their access to and from Stepan's office. The soldiers, providing corridor security checking Stepan's and Radek's identification papers, were also vetted.

Fedor was reviewing the granted formal applications for access to Government areas to the actual arrivals and who such individuals were meeting. The majority were of course Ukrainian Military personnel and senior civil servants. Fedor deleted these groups from his analysis to list the anomalies. The name of a priest, Father Andrii Polischuk, looked rather out of place. Checking the application, the access request had been made by a Miss Irina Shevchenko and authorised by a Major Aleksandr Marchuk, Head of the President's Office.

Marchuk was known to Stepan so he requested the Major to meet him in a local coffee shop. It transpired Shevchenko was engaged to a serving Flight Lieutenant in the Ukrainian Air Force flying MIG 29s. She was planning her wedding and wished like her parents to be married in St Volodymyr's Cathedral. Shevchenko had begged Marchuk to approve Father Polischuk's access to see her and in the end the Major had agreed. Stepan understood his colleague's natural difficulty if not in-built historic reluctance to see a visiting priest as a security threat.

Fedor's and Artur's research in the meantime on Father Polischuk had produced some worrisome red flags. He was born in Rostov-on-Don and had attended Moscow State Technical University. In his late twenties, Andrii married prior to attending in his early thirties the St Petersburg Orthodox Theological Academy. Bishop Kirill, as he was then before becoming Patriarch of the Russian Orthodox Church, had ordained him as priest in the early 1980s. Putin was at that time head of the KGB in St Petersburg and Polischuk was identified in photographs with both Putin and Kirill. After being ordained, he was initially a parish priest in a suburb of Kharkiv before being moved to other parishes like Brovary and Kryvyi Rih.

Was Polischuk the snake in the grass Stepan asked himself? Why did people like Marchuk and him ultimately consider a priest or any priest should be above suspicion? The Ukrainian Government had, as he knew from Top Secret Cabinet papers, been wary of acting against Ukranian Orthodox Church under the control of Moscow's Patriarch Kirill. This general reluctance emanated from not wanting to cross any lines on the freedom of religious belief, or fall foul of the European Union or other international norms in protecting an individual's right of worship. The Ukranian Government had also wanted to avoid offending the church's adherents, acutely aware that within the ranks of its priests and worshippers there were plenty of patriotic Ukrainians fighting on the frontlines against the Russians. Nevertheless, a change of heart in Government circles and across Ukraine's entire faithful happened as evidence of how Father Mykola Yevtushenko, a priest of the Ukrainian Orthodox Church, collaborated with the Russians, offering benedictions and urging his parishioners to welcome the invading forces. This 75-year-old cleric, whose trial was underway in Kyiv, stands accused of identifying locals most likely to resist Russia's savage 33-day occupation of Bucha - a suburban town just northwest of Kyiv now synonymous with Russian atrocities and war crimes. Yevtushenko had not only condoned such cruelty but also persisted in singling out local officials, Ukrainian army veterans, and the houses where wealthy people live to be looted to the occupiers. The Russians had left behind four hundred and fifty eight bodies, mostly civilians, including those of children. Victims of an occupying army bent on instilling dread through rape, murder, and shameless terror. After the withdrawal, the town was littered with bodies, some buried and others not with even mutilated corpses of men, women and children found in a basement.

Stepan was aware of legislation to protect the country's 'spiritual independence' was now before Verkhovna Rada *(Ukraine's Parliament)*. It would when ratified make it impossible for any religious organization affiliated with or influenced by Russia to function in Ukraine. Similarly, both Fedor and Artur separately made him aware of accusations of collaboration against more than thirty priests were currently under investigation by some of their secret service colleagues. These sensitive enquiries cut to the heart of a profound and highly political schism dividing the Orthodox Church between the Patriarchies of Kyiv and Moscow. The duplicity of priests like Yevtushenko aligned to Moscow's Ukrainian Orthodox Church (UOC) had become widely known. Public opinion was now firmly behind the proposed total ban on the UOC and seizure of its property making the Orthodox Church of Ukraine (OCU) the sole protector of the Orthodox Faith in the country.

Opening another link, Stepan found that the Moscow Patriarchy was established in 1943 by Joseph Stalin as the governing body to run Orthodox religious affairs in the Soviet Union. In reality, the Moscow Patriarchy was and is still a Russian state agency. The Patriarchy is a front organization of the Russian intelligence services, with its priests used as agents of influence, even for active measures and spying missions. As he accessed other files, Stepan came to the conclusion that, since the dissolution of the Soviet Union, not much has changed. The Russian Orthodox Church and UOC were one and the same used by the Kremlin as part of its subversive hybrid warfare against Ukraine since, if not before, the 2013/14 Maidan Revolution.

Why did a priest need to come to the inner sanctum of the Ukrainian Government to discuss a marriage of a secretary? It made no sense. What was Polischuk's real purpose Stepan wondered? Leaning back in his desk chair, Stepan picked up the phone to Kommidor Dmytro Koval who had absolute control of security matters within and across the Government underground complex. There was no criticism of Stepan and his team's limited investigation rather relief that apart from the information gathering meeting with Major Marchuk, no action had been taken to alert either those close to or working in the President's Secretariat or Father Andrii Polischuk or indeed anyone else. Kommidor Koval's Counter Intelligence and Internal Security Group would initially sweep the Presidential suite, offices, and Secretariat for any electronic listening devices as part of a regular but random roster. Sweeps of common areas from lavatories to canteens where often people feel uninhibited in terms of 'careless talk' would also importantly take place. Electronic bugging and surveillance of the prime if not obvious suspect, Father Andrii Polischuk would begin. Even so Koval's Security Group would take an equally close look at Irina Shevchenko who would similarly have her apartment, phone, and car bugged/tracked. Steps would also be taken to know precisely what documents, emails, and calls passed across Shevchenko's desk with Major Marchuk being replaced by one of Koval's team. For Stepan, Fedor, and Artur it was back to their day job of building the Secret Army.

Chapter 10

Ramzan Kadyrov had left President Putin's Novo-Ogaryovo residence some thirty kilometres outside Moscow angry and frustrated. Colonel-General Laskutin, Head of the GRU, had flatly denied before his President any knowledge of what Ukrainian Force had been operating within the forests of Sumy to such deadly effect in March and April. The late General Bolat Abubakarov was a close personal friend and also his daughter's godfather who had, in his words, been assassinated in Loknya. How could it be a State Security Service like the GRU could have no idea or inkling as to who the assassins were! It was not the Caucasian way to allow the deaths of a further six hundred and eighty three Chechens to go unavenged or unpunished.

Losing his temper had nevertheless resulted five weeks later in a meeting at the headquarters of the Federal Security Service (FSB) at 24 Kuznetski Most with Kirill Vasilyev and Vladimir Bogdanov, FSB Directors for Special Programmes for the President. Having been ushered into a 9th floor conference room and introductions made, Ramzan at last received the information he had been seeking for months.

'Mr President my colleague and I have established who we believe was the officer in charge of whatever Special Forces unit was operating in the Forests of Sumy, a Major Radek Król of Poland's GROM.'

Director Vasilyev passed a set of A4 sized photographs across the table to Ramzan.

'What makes the FSB and you certain that Król was responsible for the deaths of so many of my countrymen?'

Director Bogdanov continued.

'The chatter amongst the ranks was of a Special Forces Unit that had inflicted major casualties on the invaders while operating behind enemy lines. A military hospital train at that time heading to Poland had, amongst the many badly wounded Ukrainian soldiers, a Polish officer on board identified as Król. At the border, a medivac helicopter spirited away that officer for treatment.'

'Director Bogdanov that hardly confirms Król was the commanding officer of a group operating behind our front line. He could simply be a casualty of war who was caught by chance from shelling in the centre of Sumy. Similarly, with NATO being extremely cautious about not entering by mistake into direct confrontation with Russia why would Poland risk or be allowed to risk making such a mis-step.'

'Mr President, that is not for us to answer. You have asked our President for help in identifying who was responsible for the slaughter of your troops in the Forests of Sumy. We are dealing with the fog of war. Memories of even yesterday in a battle for survival are permanently lost amongst the living let alone the dead or dying. Ukrainian Soldiers, who survived the initial battles, have been in many cases been posted to the Front Lines of the Donbass and South East. Both sides have taken major casualties so finding eye witness corroboration is now nearly impossible. We can say with certainty a fully recovered Major, now Colonel Król, was in Kyiv a couple of months ago though the purpose of his visit was unclear. However there was a private dinner at the Radisson where the Colonel was the guest of honour with various Government dignitaries and the Polish Ambassador were present. A waitress, who is an FSB agent, heard during that dinner the mention of Chechens, the Forests of Sumy, and the Order of the Gold Star.'

'Mr President I am passing you details from the FSB and GRU records as to what covert activities this Polish Officer has been involved with and his reputation as a highly professional GROM soldier. Whilst we recognise your desire of accountability if not revenge, your soldiers died in battle. They were neither murdered nor killed indiscriminately for no reason. It was a 'kill or be killed' environment. Our President asks, as do we, you to reflect on such facts' added Director Vasilyev.

'Directors I thank you for the information'. Ramzan Kadyrov stood and left the 9th Floor.

Chapter 11

For Jan Chmura agreeing what security measures and upgrades needed to be taken across the Król family compound had exercised his diplomatic skills to the full. Tomek and Radek had clearly decided discretion was the better part of valour with the Król women in the mix. Alexandra, with her MI6 experience, was possibly the easier of the two ladies but Ewa Król proved a real challenge for Jan.

That said, once the works were agreed, the military contractors took full advantage of the milder late autumn weather to complete the contract. The construction of independent panic rooms and diesel generators (accessed solely from the basements to both properties) formed a major part of the security upgrade. Pressure pads were randomly installed together with powerful floodlighting in a one hundred metre arc round the buildings. These additions complimented an infra-red camera system that was movement sensitive at two hundred metres linked to an audible buzzer across each house. As for the rear woodland within a chain-link fence, this remained a weak point in the compound's security especially as beyond the property's boundary it became thick forest.

The decision was taken not to involve the local police. Drawing attention to the Król Family was something that would inevitably leak out to the media and risk details of the covert mission in the Forests of Sumy becoming common knowledge. The European Union, NATO, and other countries supporting Ukraine would undoubtedly consider Poland's action at a minimum as provocative if not foolhardy. As for the Kremlin looking for any excuse to ratchet up the conflict, it was too awful to contemplate.

Whilst Mielec's now active squadron of MQ9 Reaper *(Predator)* drones were tasked to run surveillance missions over the Krol compound during the day and more frequently at night, Alexandra, Ewa, Tomek, and Radek when he was home had to adjust to the new normal. Carrying on your day to day lives without looking over your shoulder in public or being even afraid to leave the compound had to be faced. Journeys into Niepolomice had to be more random and at different times but always in daylight. Paying attention to the surrounding environment whether checking the rear view mirror or being aware of unfamiliar faces was part of that new normal.

Although Ukraine's Southern counter-offensive had resulted in the liberation of Kherson in early November, the initial euphoria of this battlefield success began to fade as the aftermath of the Russian withdrawal became apparent. NATO's Military Committee had requested Strategic Command Europe to provide a current battlefield assessment for subsequent political consideration by the North Atlantic Council Members. Radek had joined a group of NATO's International Military Staff in Kherson at Lieutenant-General Politczek's request.

Chapter 12

I t was the last Friday of November. Lieutenant-General Politczek's 8th floor office's conference table had Colonels Chmura, Król, and Hanko waiting for the General to finish his phonecall before their weekly meeting could begin. Grzegorz hung the handset back into its cradle and walked towards the vacant chair at the head of the table.

'Radek, begin'.

'The Russian withdrawal from Kherson and the wider region to the West of the Dnipro has revealed major infrastructure damage. Unsurprisingly four key bridges across the river have been destroyed. Upstream, the Kakhovka Dam was also damaged but is now controlled by Ukrainian forces. As the Russian Army retreated to the East side of the Dnipro, there was a deliberate and systematic policy of making human civilian life within Kherson intolerable. Electricity, internet and water supply networks had been effectively blown up from substations to telecommunication towers to pumping stations - all critical infrastructure for the City to be habitable. Even Kherson's combined heat and power station has been reduced to rubble. What caused me personally some unexpected surprise was the Russian Army went as far as to exhume the remains of Grigory Potemkin, Catherine the Great's Field Marshal and lover making the looting of museums, galleries, and removal of statues have almost being given an appearance of normality.

Electricity and water repairs cannot be completed in the short term. Ukrainian Authorities have initiated efforts to facilitate voluntary evacuations of Kherson residents until the City was more secure. Government advice is that inhabitants would be better off and safer finding winter accommodation elsewhere. As such, Ukraine has taken responsibility to transport people where they wish to go. Similarly, displaced people are urged not to return to the City or Region until stabilisation measures such as de-mining and removal anti-personnel munitions have been thoroughly completed. There are already mounting civilian casualties and deaths across the recently liberated territories and settlements. It is clear the removal of mines and tripwires across the recaptured territories will take months if not years. Before the war, Kherson had some three hundred thousand inhabitants. By the end of the Russian occupation, less than eighty thousand were left. Many civilians had fled westward but close to seventy thousand were evacuated by the Russian military from Kherson to the eastern bank of the river Dnipro. Whether the 'evacuated' were forced deportations or civilians simply opting to survive whatever their politics is an open question.

Since Ukrainian Forces liberated Kherson, the City has suffered increasing daily shelling from the eastern bank of the Dnipro. If the senseless damage to Kherson was not already enough, the regrouping Russian Army artillery is sending shells, salvo after salvo, to flatten the already uninhabitable residential property whilst continuing to destroy local Government buildings. It is like watching the destruction of Mariupol in slow motion. Yet another indication the only Russian War plan is to win by attrition. After seven months of occupation, I am no longer shocked that investigators have already recorded five hundred and seventy eight acts of extreme violence against civilians. War crimes committed by Russian troops and their accomplices in Kherson and across the region to subdue the local populace through fear and intimidation is, we know from history, page one line one of Russian Strategy. '

'With the recapture of Kherson, the Ukrainians have once again control of the North Crimean Canal that supplies eighty five per cent of Crimea's drinking water and substantial irrigation for agriculture. Do you see Ukraine once more immediately restricting this supply Radek?'

'The answer is, for now, a categoric 'No'. The water through the canal in winter will not have a significant influence on the supply to Crimea, Witoria. Their reservoirs are close to full at this time of year making such a move purely symbolic. Nevertheless, in spring next year, the lack of water in the canal would create supply problems for the population and the peninsula's military bases. This makes gaining control over the Kakhovskaya hydroelectric power plant, and thus managing the North Crimean Canal, a primary military goal. Ukraine's Military is not yet in a position to begin, in my view, its counter-offensive strikes earlier than Spring 2023. It is all very well for political messaging to Putin and Russia that the West is united and will support Ukraine for the long haul to regain its territory goals. Nevertheless, the step by step approach by NATO is understandable yet why have the members seemingly forgotten Russia invaded Ukraine? Russia only responds to ultimate aggressive force. My NATO military colleagues have very similar views that regaining occupied territory cannot be achieved without heavy armour and artillery together with offensive air support from helicopter gunships to modern fighter jets. Before any talk of peace negotiations, the war has to be won on the battlefield.'

'What do you think I should be telling the Prime Minister, Minister of Defence, and the other members of the Security Committee on Monday afternoon Radek.'

'The Russians are regrouping. Our intelligence, confirmed by the Pentagon, has established Russia is receiving arms from Iran and North Korea. In addition, even China is now surreptitiously, to avoid being caught by secondary sanctions, providing advanced computer chips amongst other things. Conscripts are unsurprisingly merely gun fodder on the battlefield with more mobilisations expected. Yevgeny Prigozhin's Wagner mercenaries, with eighty per cent or more recruited from Russian penal colonies, are now actively involved on the battlefront. Furthermore, Ukraine is being systematically turned into dust by long range missiles fired from the safety of Russian airspace and the Black Sea. Would any NATO member also stand for its Capital City and citizens being mercilessly targeted by such barbarians and its towns made uninhabitable without responding? It is no different than a boxer being told to fight with one hand tied behind his back. Anyone in the military knows combined land and air with mobility is the strategy to break the frontline deadlock of trench warfare. The Ukrainians need, amongst other things, heavy armour. For example, all the European NATO members have German made Leopard II battle-tanks. A tank far superior to anything the Russian Army has or indeed the Ukrainians have. Both militaries are still equipped with Soviet Era tanks. It is simply not good enough for Poland or others to donate obsolete equipment. Neither is it acceptable to use maintenance and training as an excuse for dithering and delay – this only assists the enemy, Russia'

'Jan, do you agree?'

'Yes General. There are over two thousand Leopard tanks within NATO and in Europe. Ukrainians tank crews will need to be trained but the tanks are diesel powered, relatively easy to maintain, and servicing nodes for repair can be established. Poland has some two hundred and fifty Leopards so we can be generous. My German colleagues in the Bundeswehr confirm the manufacturer is ready to add another production line plus provide servicing and parts back up. President Zelensky has asked initially for a hundred Leopards. Our General Staff and the Ukrainian High Command consider at least three hundred for the counter-offensive with rapid replacement of losses are necessary for a Spring offensive. Our Government and NATO have to stop acting as if the West wants simply a World War I style battlefront and provide the heavy armour, heavy artillery, and ground attack air support from helicopter gunships to combat fighter aircraft for Ukraine to win. Talk of providing the aggressor with an off-ramp by trading Ukraine's territory is untenable morally.'

'Jan is correct. Ukraine has since the 2014 been incorporating NATO organisational standards into its Army and other military arms. The intention is to have the battlefield interoperability necessary to make membership or initially an associate status like Finland and Sweden possible. Clearly, when victory over the Russians is achieved, it may be full membership becomes the only option in the peace negotiations for Ukraine's ultimate territorial security from Russia and Belarus. However such debate is for the future. Today we have stop Ukraine feeling like a second class citizen only fit for NATO members' obsolete kit from tanks to planes so far donated. The resolution of its civilian population suffering power blackouts and a military having shown Russian Army for what it is *(a propaganda led paper tiger)* deserve the best and latest battlefield equipment.'

'Thank you Witoria. Presumably, you are all thinking for gunships and planes Lockheed Martin's Apache and F-16 respectively?'

There was a murmur of agreement round the table from the Colonels before Jan spoke.

'General, we have all witnessed the Apache's offensive capability in Afghanistan whether engaging ground targets such as enemy infantry, military vehicles, and fortifications. It also provides direct and accurate close air support for ground troops and of course an anti-tank role to destroy grouped enemy armour. The Apache carries an array of weapon systems including autocannons, machine guns, rockets, and anti-tank missiles such as the Hellfire plus a capability to carry air-to-air missiles. As for Lockheed Martin's F-16, it is a compact multi-role fighter aircraft that is highly manoeuvrable and proven in air-to-air combat and air-to-surface attack. The F-16's combat radius *(distance it can fly to enter air combat, stay, fight and return)* exceed that of all potential threat fighter aircraft. In an air-to-surface role, the F-16 can fly more than eight hundred and sixty kilometres, deliver its weapons payload with superior accuracy, defend itself against Russian MIGs and SUKHOIs, and return to its starting point. With an all-weather capability to accurately deliver ordnance during non-visual bombing conditions, it is the ideal fighter along with the Apache helicopter gunships to support the Ukrainian Army's breakout counter-offensive. The speedy supply of these aircraft moves Ukraine towards regaining its occupied territory in 2023 and ultimately peace. I would stress the provision of this advanced weaponry is to enable the Ukrainians to further defend themselves against a barbaric enemy not to attack Moscow.'

'Witoria, what information do we have on Russia's next moves on the battlefield?'

'General, our intelligence indicates that, by the February 24th anniversary in 2023, there will be extreme pressure politically for a battlefield success. Prigozhin's Wagner mercenaries are increasingly involved in close quarter fighting in and around Soledar along with the Russian Army. There seems to be no account being taken for the lives of its soldiers by the Russian High Command as wave after wave are slaughtered. The small salt mining town does not have strategic battlefield significance so the expectation is for a tactical withdrawal sometime in January. Nevertheless, Colonel-General Sergey Surovikin's time as

Commander of all Forces in Ukraine is, I believe, limited even though he was only appointed in early October. My reasoning is simply, in a televised meeting with Russian defence minister, Sergei Shoigu, Surovikin, made public his recommendation for the withdrawal of Russian forces from Kherson to save Russian troops. President Putin does not want to hear bad news even though Surovikin (known as General Armageddon from his brutal and ruthless actions in Syria) was correct militarily in recommending such a decision. Our and NATO's intelligence sources sense another reshuffle to bolster the army's sagging war effort while contending with the Wagner Group's growing influence and interference on the battlefield. Prigozhin is becoming increasingly vocal about the poor performance of the Russian Army alongside even pro-Putin supporters voicing similar dissent. Kadyrov is also in the wings of Kremlin politics albeit a less vociferous critic. Both men are seeking to be in the political mix if not as a successor to President Putin then gaining greater power in supporting his ultimate replacement. This gathering storm within Kremlin circles is why Putin needs in the coming months, if not around the first anniversary of his so-called Special Military Operation, some successes on the battlefield to silence these critics. Surovikin has begun, we learn, to improve the command and control structure across the occupied territories with intense fighting in and around Bakhmut. Satellite imagery is yet to show for now a build-up of Russian Forces sufficient in men materials and equipment to launch an effective counter offensive against the Ukrainian Army whether from the North East, Donbass, or Southern fronts. Belarus still remains a conundrum as to whether it will be a base for another military thrust to take Kyiv or continue to be a launch pad for missiles. This rather highlights in my view the battlefield stalemate at present and the urgent requirement for heavy armour, heavy artillery, and fighter aircraft together with helicopter gunships for Ukraine's military. Western politicians need to step up from rhetoric, whatever it takes, to fulfilling that promise. Russia's performance has exposed its military's lack of readiness and inability of air ground integration. Bearing in mind the modernisation undertaken since 2008 and sums expended, it also highlights again our intelligence shortcomings in completely underestimating the depth of corruption in Russia's procurement let alone quality control.

Iranian drones continue along with cruise and other Russian missiles to inflict even more serious damage to Ukraine's energy grid. Notwithstanding the somewhat frosty relations between Ukraine and Israel because of its failures to condemn Russia's invasion and to provide a similar air defence system to 'Iron Dome', we have an indication that Ukrainian Secret Service and Mossad are planning something against Iran. Our best guess is the destruction of the Iranian Drone Manufacturing base, in part or whole.'

'Witoria please remind me why Israel has only sent humanitarian aid so far and a field hospital?'

'General, Israel's regional security over the skies has been enhanced since Russia actively supported militarily Bashir Assad's Syrian regime. Russia has enabled the Israeli Air Force to fly missions against Hamas targets whether in Lebanon or Syria without fear of engaging the Russian or Syrian Air Forces. This arrangement has made Israel take a more measured line in its sanguine decision not to send military aid to Ukraine or join Western sanctions against

Russia. Support for Ukraine though, thanks to continued United States pressure, is increasing with air defence systems at last being provided together with artillery shells from US stockpiles within Israel.'

Grzegorz stood up and walked to the windows of his office. He lit a cigarette and took a long first draw before exhaling. Turning round to face his senior subordinates, he began to summarise his thoughts.

'We forget all too easily with today's media coverage why Poland and other countries are resisting Russian aggression. The International Rules based order established in the aftermath of World War II demanded respect for human rights, international law, and national sovereignty. Seizing your neighbour's land by force, destroying people's homes, and deporting children into the depths of Siberia are not acts that accept another country's right to self-determination.

From today's discussion, we are talking about the Ramstein Contact Group providing Ukraine with whatever it takes to win. It also has to deliver militarily the air-defence capabilities to protect Ukrainian citizens and critical infrastructure. In addition, long range precision strikes against command headquarters and logistic nodes have to be made achievable, apart from isolating Crimea making it untenable for the Russian Army to remain. The Ramstein Contact Group has to deny Russian sanctuary in the border hinterland and provide the longer range missiles for HIMARS for example. Ukraine's military also has to have the equipment to conduct mobile operations. These are the necessary capabilities to win.

At my Monday meeting with the Prime Minister at the Cabinet Security Committee, I will stress the need for all politicians to match the will of the Ukrainians in this fight. We have to stop overthinking what the Kremlin may or may not do and live up to the statement whatever it takes. History reminds me of the Warsaw Uprising in 1944 when the Russians could have stopped what became a senseless slaughter. The Red Army waited on the right bank of the Vistula River and watched some two hundred thousand civilians on the left bank being brutally murdered. The corollary is NATO's similar indifference, similar to Russia's actions back in 1944, in not providing offensive capabilities to Ukraine. TV screens across the World show unsurprisingly after Grozny and Aleppo the daily loss of civilian life – we cannot and must not be indifferent to such slaughter that includes now thousands of children. The West's political will must finally match Ukraine's defiance to win.'

Chapter 13

Pawel Nowak was an orderly in Jana Pawla II hospital and an embedded sleeper agent of Russia's FSB. His handler had now instructed him to establish the name and home address of an injured Polish Officer who was airlifted in mid-April for emergency surgery. He remembered the rotating military armed guard permanently outside the officer's room and in the corridor ensuring no unauthorised access. Pawel also recalled chatter amongst nurses and doctors at the Ward Nurse's Station that a highly decorated Special Forces officer's life was hanging by a thread after hours of surgery. Pawel had filed a report to his handler but had received no further request for information. His handler, like him, assumed at that time the injuries occurred on a local military exercise.

The cigarette smoke filled café at the junction of Prospekt Mira and Krasnoflotskaja Streets in Grozny was the designated meeting place for an FSB officer to hand over that information to Musa Usumov, a high ranking official within Ramzan Kadyrov's inner circle.

In ABW's Intelligence Monitoring Department, Colonel Hanko was called by one of the 'dark net and web' surveillance operators to view a posting -

A bounty of eight million United States dollars has been placed on the life of a senior Polish Officer. The funds are already deposited in a Swiss Bank account awaiting only satisfactory proof of death for their immediate release. Encrypted details including photographs and locational details are available in a remote data room and a negotiated upfront payment for expenses will be considered. Only those with serious interest and the provable skills to complete this task should make initial contact via the browser to this website

Chapter 14

The General read the dark net posting. Quite clearly, Kadyrov had decided a professional assassin delivered a far more clinical result. Furthermore, why pass the mission to some of his fighters? A merciless perseverance and brutality may well be attributes on the battlefield but they lacked the finesse and certainty of a kill by a professional assassin. This meant that three or four of World's most competent individual assassins would be attracted to such a contract. Protecting and defending Radek and his close family would be more than a challenge when there is no indication of the timing of any attack or indeed where such an assault might take place. Nevertheless, he had instructed Colonel Hanko to provide a list of the most probable assassins as a first step to putting a name and face to the likely assassin. Grzegorz left his office and walked towards Radek's office in the knowledge this was hardly the news anyone would wish to hear in the week before Christmas Eve.

Nineteen hundred miles away in Barcelona's warm winter sunshine, Peter van de Berg sipped a double espresso on a table outside Dalston Coffee in Les Ramelleres. He had followed up on the dark net posting and was beginning to review the information in the data room. His target was a GROM Special Forces officer now holding a senior position within ABW, Poland's counter espionage agency. The man called Radek Król had seemingly a chest full of medals from successful missions. Aerial photos of Rakowiecka Street and surrounding buildings together the man's home in Niepolomice provided a base of information. There were plans of the houses within what appeared to be a family compound together with various photos of the occupants including a number of St Bernard dogs. Before accepting the contract, he mailed the website for clarification as to whether the sole target was the officer or if collateral family were also to be targeted, the time allowed for the kill and a request for fifty per cent of the contract sum to be paid into one of his designated accounts if he was to proceed. Peter van de Berg was a Dutchman who had many pseudonyms as he had criss-crossed borders executing contracts. However, in the exclusive underworld of professional assassins Peter was known as 'the Surgeon' for his clinical and methodical executions.

Grzegorz knew that a meticulous assassin was very hard threat to neutralise. It was no different to a fanatic totally unknown to the authorities carrying out an act of terror. Poland was not China where the Intelligence Services had the assistance of facial recognition technology. Indeed, even if such a facility was available to the Security Services, could major intelligence agencies like the CIA, BND, DGSE, MI6, Mossad and other Western Agencies even put faces to such high-end assassins? Kadyrov had clearly thought through how best to achieve Chechen revenge for the deaths of his country's soldiers in the Forests of Sumy. A Caucasian would not stand out amongst the Polish population and could easily travel unnoticed once within the Schengen area.

Chapter 15

Rakowiecka Street Headquarters of ABW was a hive of activity leading up to the eighth meeting of the Ukraine Defence Contact Group being held on January 20th at Ramstein Air Base in Germany. As previously, senior defence and military officials from over fifty countries, including NATO members, would be taking decisions that would both shape and determine the course of Russia's war of aggression against Ukraine in 2023; possibly beyond if major offensive and air defence capabilities were not approved. For months, Western countries had been rebuffing urgent Ukrainian requests to send heavy tanks, such as the American M1 Abrams, the German Leopard and the British Challenger 2. The British government had already broken ranks and confirmed Challenger 2s would be sent to Ukraine. Importantly, whilst attending the World Economic Forum in Davos Switzerland, the Prime Minister in a CNN interview had made it clear that Poland wanted and was ready to send Leopards subject to Germany agreeing to their export to Ukraine. When asked Poland's reaction if such consent was not forthcoming, the response was simply, with a group of like-minded countries, the tanks would be exported anyway.

Whilst Ukraine needed tanks in particular to break through the Russian lines, Washington and Berlin continued to argue respectively that the Abrams was inappropriate for the battlefield citing fuel and maintenance issues and the Leopards would escalate further future relations with Russia. This disagreement continued at Ramstein inspite of countries like Poland, Finland, France and others within the support group demanding that the United States as leader of the West together with Germany enabled the delivery of tanks. By January 25th, International Political Pressure and internal pressure within both the Biden and Schulz administrations meant a policy pivot with Abrams and Leopard tanks going to Ukraine.

Along with tanks, Ukraine needs defensive weapons that can counter Russia's bombardment from the air. The deadly attacks on large cities showed that Russia had no compunction about using inaccurate ballistic missiles armed with heavy warheads against Ukrainian civilians. Radek was left to deal with, in conjunction with Poland's Military, the logistics of two Patriot batteries designated for Poland being sent to Ukraine instead. A task not quite as simple as it sounded as, apart from training Ukrainian personnel in Poland, repairs and maintenance systems had to be put in place plus their ultimate transportation to the city or cities designated by Ukraine. He was also dealing with the initial fourteen Leopard II tanks to be delivered after Ukrainian tank crews had been suitably trained. Świdnik military base in Eastern Poland was chosen because of its proximity to a railhead and the Ukrainian border. Allocating this task to Radek had been deliberate by the Lieutenant-General, he had to be kept busy without having time to consider the sword of Damocles hanging over him and those he loved.

His protection on zero information on the assassination threat had become Colonel Jan Chmura's responsibility. Whilst the Król properties within the compound were almost a kilometre from the rest of Niepolomice, local police had conducted a census of those nearby properties establishing ownership, occupants, and any vacant units during January. The empty properties were checked as to lines of sight into the Król compound for a sniper. Two buildings were found to meet that requirement for a sniper shooting from such deep cover. Similarly, five occupied properties by local residents had similar potential.

This survey had been conducted under the guise of an environmental protection scheme to protect development expansion into green spaces. The real estate agency in the centre of the village was on notice to advise the Local Police of any new lettings or sales on a fortnightly basis. The Police were then authorised to forward the details immediately to Colonel Chmura's office.

Witoria Hanko had had to decide from the limited hard information from Western Intelligence sources on the most likely names selected by Kadyrov to assassinate Radek and probably his nearest and dearest as well.

Valentin Konnikov was a former Russian Spetsnaz sergeant who after two tours in Syria had retired from active service placed his sniper skills for hire. Now in his early forties, the CIA and Mossad credited him with various kills of Latin American politicians, business people and journalists over the last decade. His whereabouts were unknown and the only available photograph was taken fifteen years ago for his military personnel records.

Jean-Paul Moreau was a former South African Police sniper who had disappeared from Cape Town shortly after the millennium. His speciality seemed to be house invasion with close quarter execution. DGSE (the French Intelligence Service) and CNI (the Spanish National Intelligence Service) believed that he was responsible for specific political assassinations across Africa and the Middle East. Those kills demonstrated extreme prejudice and violence including torture. A twenty year old somewhat grainy photograph gave no clue as to what the man looked like in 2023.

All the agencies considered 'the Surgeon' as probably the most likely choice. Konnikov operated freely within Latin America. Surely he would see greater risk of detection without his support and trusted network by taking on a contract in Europe? Moreau could face similar challenges and as attractive as the contract sum, why leave sunshine for Poland's winter? Neither Konnikov nor Moreau seemingly needed money given their attributed kills so Hanko believed these assassins for hire would pass Kadyrov's opportunity. 'The Surgeon' was believed to be Dutch though there was no evidence to confirm his nationality. It would seem from the kills in differing countries across Europe, Scandinavia, and Russia the man had also skills of disguise and languages. Analysing each assassination Hanko detected a thoroughness of planning so as to select the right time and place. This meant not only spending time assessing optimal places to execute the contract but also the habits of the target or targets influencing that selection. 'The Surgeon' also planned meticulously his exit so he was never detected. The assassin was a ghost with his presence always unseen. What made Hanko firm up her view, although the scant intelligence information was leading her in that direction, was MI6's firm belief that Russia's FSB had employed 'the Surgeon' for Vladimir Muganov's execution outside Moscow in his country retreat's sauna, Boris Berezovsky's murder who was found hanged in the bathroom of his Ascot home, and Scot Young impaled on iron railings after he purportedly fell from the fourth floor of his girlfriend's flat in Marylebone.

Matt Elliott, a Major in MI6 and known to her personally from a short tumultuous love affair in 2018, was one of Radek's closest friends. Elliott had sent her an encrypted copy of a 2019 'Top Secret' MI5 Report to the Cabinet Office Briefing Rooms known as COBRA. In summary, the Report had raised major concerns about a series of suspicious deaths of businessmen. Young, a Scottish Property developer, had deep business connections to several Russian oligarchs, who had fled to the Britain because they had fallen out of favour with President Putin. The United Kingdom was perceived as a safe place to hold their wealth whether in property, stocks, or cash. The CIA had strong suspicions that these unexplained deaths on British soil were carried out by FSB agents and in specific cases by an assassin known only as 'the Surgeon'. This information had been passed onto the Government at the highest levels. The British Cabinets of whatever political colour had been reluctant to take these suspected Russian assassinations seriously. Governments in Europe and the United States had been, since Putin came to power, extremely anxious to court him in the hopes that Russia could be brought into the institutional alliances that underpinned the stability of the Western liberal world order. This did of course result in close cooperation on the war on terror and Russia playing a leading role in the Iran nuclear deal, apart from making the G7 become G8 with Russia's inclusion into this Western Club. In addition, with Europe's growing dependency on Russian Energy and money flows into financial centres, especially into the City of London, Governments felt *'why pick a fight with the Kremlin?'* over what seemed to be isolated and unproven incidents. On such reasoning, the opportunity to build a lasting alliance with Russia should not be put at risk. Another horrendous example of Britain turning a blind eye to Russia's actions was the eight year wait for Sir Robert Owen's Public Inquiry into the case of the former FSB officer Alexander Litvinenko, who died in 2006 from radiation poisoning. The most significant statement to come out of the report was Sir Robert's 2016 summary *'Taking full account of all the evidence and analysis available to me, I find that the FSB operation to kill Litvinenko was probably approved by Mr Patrushev and also by President Putin'*. Nikolai Patrushev was then head of Russia's main intelligence agency, the FSB, at the time of the murder and today he is still also within Putin's inner circle, *the Siloviki.*

The United Kingdom Government's watershed moment was though the 2018 attack against Sergei and Yulia Skripal in Salisbury with a chemical nerve agent, Novichok. It was the first time a nerve agent has been used on European soil since the Second World War endangering the lives of hundreds of innocent civilians in Britain. The British government belatedly realized that the Russian campaign of assassinations had just been allowed to spin out of control. Novichok is a highly conspicuous Russian poison, which was developed by the Soviets and is known to Western intelligence as only originating in Russia. That attack finally left no doubts as who the perpetrators were. Putin, the Report also stated, never intended to enter the liberal fold or honestly to cooperate with Western Governments. Elliott highlighted in his covering mail that Putin had been waging, since his rise to power, a covert war of subversion against Western institutions and dissidents residing in the West. In his view, after ignoring the 2014 first invasion wakeup call, the February 24th 2022 Special Military Operation put the debate beyond any reasonable doubt - the price of appeasement, as history has shown, is far too steep. Witoria agreed.

As she considered the details of the attributed murders of Muganov, Berezovsky, Young and two others in the United Kingdom to 'the Surgeon', it seemed the assassin tailored the tools of the kill to the target. This meant casting doubt on the cause of death except where head shots from close or long range were apparent. Kadyrov would obviously have asked his high level contacts in the FSB as who was the 'go to guy' for this particular assassination contract. Witoria no longer had any uncertainties as to who the assassin of choice would be, 'The Surgeon'.

Chapter 16

Airports, railway stations, and other transport nodes were places to be avoided unless there was no other option as far as Peter van de Berg was concerned. Surveillance cameras are constantly monitoring travellers day and night. His United Kingdom contracts had risked him being unnecessarily exposed in his own mind notwithstanding the precautions he had taken. This had led him to prefer accepting contracts on the European mainland where personal road transport was the safer option, albeit not without camera hazards in motorway service stations, at toll booths, or from integrated police traffic management systems.

Domaine Fleurs des Bougainvillees was a typical residential community sitting in the hillsides above Nice on the Cote d'Azur. Most of the houses had been individually designed for or by their affluent owners whether they were locals or French or from elsewhere in the Europe. Few properties ever came available and Peter had acquired his villa from the Trustees of a Swiss Banker's Estate a decade earlier. It was from here that he would plan the first part of his visit to Poland.

Having received confirmation that fifty per cent of the contract monies were now in one of his Swiss accounts in

Lugano and further half a million dollars would be paid for each close family member whether collateral damage or deliberate execution, Kadyrov's contract was accepted with a completion date of on or before April 30th.

Whether his assumption was correct or not, 'the Surgeon' saw little if any point going to Warsaw. Spending time looking for a security weakness in or around ABW's Rakowiecka Headquarters or then finding an appropriate hideout for the 'kill' shot were on the 'too hard to do' pile. Even if successful, escape would be problematic and he would be passing up a further two and a half million dollars. The assassinations would be in or around the Król compound when there would be a reasonable expectation of them all being present. Checking the diary for Polish National Holidays, April 9th had to be the date – sometime in those twenty four hours of Easter Sunday!

If Peter was to fully understand the layout of the Król compound, the immediate neighbourhood, and Niepolomice itself, the surveillance would require time. This meant a credible reason for his presence in the coming weeks and months including then formulating his plan of attack. Looking up the town of Niepolomice on his browser, there was a fourteenth century Royal Castle that was clearly the main tourist attraction, the hunting lodge of Poland's kings. 'The Surgeon' now had the seeds of an idea as to why he could become an accepted face in and around the town for weeks together with potentially an acceptable non-threatening disguise warding off, if not dismissing greater scrutiny. Whilst the dark net advertisement may well have drawn him and other assassins to the table, it had also made his task more difficult. His targets were now on notice that at any time day or night an assassin's bullet or worse could abruptly bring their lives to a violent end.

Chapter 17

Professor Lars Andersson, on sabbatical from Lund University's Faculty of Architecture, parked his Volvo Estate in the town centre of Niepolomice. Stretching after his drive, he made his way through the cars to WOŹNIAK Real Estate. Ten days before, a Secretary had contacted the agency about the availability of houses or flats to rent in the town, preferably furnished and with no restriction on a dog being allowed on the premises. It was not long before the letting staff produced a furnished house on the edge of the village overlooking open fields to a couple of properties in the distance then forest, ideal for a dog owner! Whilst the Professor was likely to only need the house for 3 months, the owner had insisted on a six month letting. After some attempts at negotiation, the Secretary for Lund University had accepted a six month letting with all the rent paid in advance. Faxes were exchanged and funds were credited to the Agency's relevant client account. A smartly dressed man, seemingly in his late fifties, sporting a beard and wearing a herringbone suit entered the Agency. It was Professor Andersson to collect the keys.

It had not been difficult for Peter to find amongst Lund's Faculty of Architecture a secretary in need of money. Astrid Johansson was pregnant from a one night stand with a Visiting Lecturer from the Czech Republic. She was determined to keep the child. However, keeping her job to pay the rent, buy food, and meet the needs of a young baby would be an ever increasing problem. Peter disguised not as the Professor or himself but as a german businessman, Hans Fischer, in a dark blue Boss suit with a white shirt matching blue tie and glasses, offering three hundred thousand kroner was impossible for her to resist. He also gave her a burner phone with the request to contact him if any enquiries were made about a Lars Andersson. In any event, she was to respond to any such a call that, as far as she knew, the Professor was researching the architectural history of certain Danish and Polish castles. For this additional service, Astrid would receive fifty thousand kroner per month with a bonus after three months sufficient to rent an apartment for many years or even buy a home in a good neighbourhood. Perhaps desperation brings strange bedfellows but for the first time in many weeks Astrid slept peacefully, her future assured financially.

Two well-trained golden retrievers began to be seen around the town with this middle aged man visiting and photographing the Royal Castle. Whilst Peter was both fluent in Swedish and Polish, in talking to people he would often deliberately begin the conversation in Swedish before checking himself to switch into Polish. This provided an excellent means gradually to become part of the local scenery. In addition, Peter would be seen with his dogs in the early morning heading to the forest and again in the late afternoon, passing the Król compound. At first this led to lots of noise from the St Bernards but as weeks passed their interest waned. Similarly, when passing the gate or walking along the boundary, there were occasional opportunities to engage an ABW chauffeur waiting for Peter's target or speak briefly to Alexandra and Tomek Król. As regards the latter, this led to an outwardly friendly hand wave on his part. In addition, if they happened to bump into one another whilst shopping in the town to engage in an impromptu conversation. Each morning after dog walking, the Professor would spend time in the Royal Palace Museum engaging its Director on particular aspects of its history like the restoration of the formal gardens. The archives were even for Peter, an interesting treasure trove of historic royal and papal documents whilst the gallery of medieval oil paintings brought to life the hunting lodge as it must have been in the fourteenth century.

Jan Chmura received, some eight days after Professor Andersson collected the keys to one of the two vacant properties overlooking the Król compound, a formal notice of the letting. The letting agent forwarded details of the faxes and a still photo taken from the security video. Jan then phoned the Lund University number have checked on his browser the phone numbers matched. Having asked the switchboard to be put through to the Rector, Astrid Johansson answered the call. She then confirmed Professor Andersson was taking a sabbatical to research the architectural history of Danish and Polish castles. Jan enquired why the Professor's name was not listed as being amongst the current teaching staff to which Astrid responded because for this year's semesters, he is on sabbatical. Once the call ended, Astrid spoke to Hans Fischer. That evening, two local police officers visited him. Apparently, there had been a series of house robberies and they wished to check the property for any signs of an attempted burglary. The Professor welcomed them asking if they wanted a hot tea as it was already extremely cold outside, minus eight. They declined. He returned to the dining room table full of assorted papers, reference books, and laptop while the officers made the pretence of checking all the external windows and doors. Some twenty minutes later, they left noting that the Professor seemed more engrossed in his papers than the police presence. Peter phoned Astrid the following morning whilst walking the dogs suspicious that an electronic bug or bugs could have been planted by the police the night before. Her earlier call had enabled him to set the scene in terms of spreading research paperwork on that dining room table just as one might envisage any Professor would haphazardly work on a research project. Peter had deliberately chosen retrievers for the contract. The breed is well-known for a playful approach to life yet gentleness with children and friendliness to other pets and strangers. He did momentarily wonder about having just one animal but decided that two would place him particularly as a non-threatening in people's sub-conscious, especially the authorities and even his targets.

Maybe Jan Chmura should have made further inquiries about the Professor. However, the introduction of a three-shift system of work at the MAN truck factory in the local industrial zone had created a steady influx of new people to be added for vetting. Hence, did a late fifties Swedish Professor merit realistically further consideration as being the potential threat when 'the Surgeon' could be living anywhere from Krakow to a village in between? Furthermore, Andersson appeared a dedicated academic spending time daily at the Royal Palace and the Lund University had rented a furnished property for his short stay in Niepolomice.

Chapter 18

The Prime Minister welcomed Lieutenant-General Politczek into his inner office. Although Poland's Security Committee would be meeting on Monday, President Zelensky's February 8th trip to meet the UK Prime Minister, Rishi Sunak, and then a late dinner with President Macron and the German Chancellor, Olaf Scholz yesterday had made him anxious for an immediate update on the politics delaying the transfer of MiG 29s to the Ukrainian Military.

'Grzegorz you will have seen on Breaking News details of Volodymyr's whistle stop tour to London, Paris, and now Brussels. Whilst I am delighted Britain is supplying longer range missiles amongst a further armaments and munitions package, Sunak echoed a previous comment by Macron that combat planes along with everything else are still capable of being delivered. However, what we all know in supporting Ukraine's War Effort with advanced equipment from tanks to planes, the training period for tank crews and aviators rather than delivery is the present holdup in bringing such squadrons to the front. Similarly, whilst much talk has been made about combat aircraft, the British have F-35s and Typhoons whilst the French fly Mirages so interoperability will become an issue. I think Sunak's decision to begin training now Ukrainian flyers on NATO standard planes makes sense but it will still take time, certainly six months. He has certainly shown the way for all NATO members to follow suit including ourselves. Nevertheless, I can foresee increasing pressure on us simply to handover our twenty eight operational MiGs so where are we?'

'Prime Minister, our MiG-29s were updated to NATO standards in cooperation with Israel Aerospace Industries but their service life is coming to an end. All these aircraft will be totally replaced between 2024 and 2026 by the F-35 Lighting II. So the Polish Air Force has an ageing and airworthy fleet of fighters that are already familiar to Ukrainian aviators. The Russian Air Forces has failed to achieve air superiority. Hence, the shipment of our combat ready fighters would further bolster the operational effectiveness of the Ukrainian Air Force. Yet delivering combat aircraft is a serious contribution to any Nation at war by a neutral NATO state, even if not embroiled in face to face conflict. The Russian Defence Ministry has drawn the line between being non-neutral and hostile, stating that the latter would be considered if an external state allows the Ukrainian Air Force shelter in neutral airbases. This means the departure of such aircraft in full combat mode *(ie armed and tanked)* from the neutral state to Russia or occupied territories piloted by the Ukrainians would be considered non-neutral and hostile ie unsurprisingly cross-border flights do cross that red line for Russia and NATO. Although I am no Lawyer, the Laws of Neutrality and Air Warfare with regard to shipment of military aircraft by a neutral state to a belligerent state like Ukraine are too ambiguous and politically impacted to be a part of customary International Law, especially when the beneficiary of such help is a victim of outright aggression in total breach of the International Rules based Order of the United Nations Charter. Therefore, it is completely permissible to deliver the combat aircraft, component parts, and ammunition to any victim of aggression but not to engage in direct combat if one is to remain neutral according to the Law and Practice..'

'What else should I consider in making this step?'

'Prime Minister, the United States has already committed months ago to backfill immediately F-35s so Poland's and NATO's Eastern Security will not be compromised by the transfer of the MiG-29s. Our Pilots have already been on a rolling training programme since we contracted for the F-35s back in 2020. Initially, with the United States Air Force in Columbus Air Force Base (AFB) Mississippi, Vance AFB Oklahoma, Laughlin AFB Texas and now finally in Ramstein. As for the MiGs, the Ukrainian pilots will need some training on the NATO interoperability avionics with ground forces but we are, I understand, talking about a matter of one or two weeks.'

'Thank you Grzegorz your summary of the status quo is most helpful. Before I leave for the Council in Brussels, I feel you have something else to say?'

'Yes Prime Minister, it is clear to me that Zelensky is using the British as the stalking horse for the United States and some NATO members to stop this incremental approach. It is about winning and I am frustrated by politicians coming out with statements like *whatever it takes and as long as it takes*. I remind you of my input to your Monday Security Committee a few weeks back. We, by which I mean the

United States, NATO, and others in the fifty members Ramstein coalition, have to provide Ukraine with capabilities – the tools to win the war. We have to provide the capabilities to deny Russia its present advantages of Sanctuary and Mass in respect of artillery and infantry. This means precision longer range missiles to destroy command Headquarters, transportation infrastructure, and munition centres. Talking to our Military Strategists, even if Mariupol and other ports are liberated on the Sea of Azov, they will be unable to function with Crimea dominating the Kerch Straits. Even if Ukraine is able to recover the Donbass, Odesa can still be shelled some three hundred kilometres away from Crimea. There will be no peace. For me Crimea has to be the key. Thus the Ukrainian Army needs longer range precision weapons to make Crimea untenable for the Russians first and then deal with the Donbass. The West has to get busy and stop swallowing Russian propaganda. Do we really believe half million troops have been mobilised and trained with helmets, boots, winter clothing, housing, and food? Precision defeats mass – no shells for artillery or bullets for its untrained infantry! It is so obvious what Ukraine needs yesterday and fighter jets are, in my opinion, not a priority until Ukraine has effective air defence. Similarly, the inference of fresh attacks from Belarus and Russia are a propaganda distraction for Ukraine's High Command if the West's combined intelligence is correct. The disconnection to capabilities is the West's step by step approach whereby delivery operationally to the front takes months. Russia has to be defeated on the battlefield and removed completely from Ukrainian pre 2014 territory. Anything less will just allow Russia to rebuild its forces and come back again in two or three years when World War III will happen. All this political and diplomatic dancing round the Christmas Tree and shilly-shallying while we see more Ukrainian civilians senselessly killed does not sit well with me, let alone nightly seeing towns turned into rubble.'

'Does this mean you see F-16s now as nice to have as opposed to need to have?'

'No Prime Minister, fighter aircraft are needed to support combined mechanised heavy armour and mobile infantry defensive and offensive counter attacks. The problem is we should have been training Ukrainian pilots months ago. We are back to that disconnect similarly to tank crews having to understand Leopards. Nevertheless, fighters require logistics support from maintenance to munitions to the rescue of downed pilots. This will have to be established in-country first before any fighters are delivered. Less we forget, attack helicopters are also a priority – let's start to be ahead before Zelensky asks for such kit!'

'Grzegorz I do not disagree. Our Baltic and Scandinavian friends, like us, have no illusions about the Russians. Thank you for this early morning briefing on the way to Frederic Chopin. By the way how is Colonel Król?'

'You mean since having a target placed on his back by Kadyrov ... *(seeing the Prime Minister nod the General continued)* ... at the moment Król is spending the majority of his time in Mielec and nearby military bases firefighting the issues arising from multiple deliveries daily of armaments for Ukraine. We are keeping him very busy so his return visits to the family home in Niepolomice are sporadic and unplanned. From his family's viewpoint, they are safer when Radek is not home and likewise Radek is for now safer on a military base.'

'Grzegorz, with heavy armour and mechanised infantry vehicles now being supplied by all of NATO, are the railway spurs at the 1520mm gauge now operational at the new military border crossings?'

'Yes Prime Minister - rapid flatbed loading at the new railheads is finally operational.'

At that moment, the Prime Minister's limousine came to a halt. The passenger door was held open by one of his protection team as he dashed up the steps for the flight to Brussels. Grzegorz was left in his own thoughts as he was chauffeured back to Rakowiecka Street. Was Witoria Hanko correct that the Kadyrov's assassin would be 'the Surgeon'? Was the man or woman already in Niepolomice observing the Króls? Had ABW done enough to protect Radek and his family?

Chapter 19

The major problem facing Poland was the ever increasing supplies of armaments and munitions arriving daily at Mielec and two other nearby military bases. It was a logistics nightmare. Shipments by Galaxy, Hercules, and other military transports from other thirty countries contained not only munitions, parts, and spares for previously supplied armaments but also ever increasing deliveries of new advanced weapons and systems. The administrative and coordination tasks were a daily 24/7 logistics challenge for everyone involved with road and rail shipments added into the mix. When the supply to the Eastern and Southern fronts is around fifteen hundred kilometres distant, servicing battlefront requirements daily from such inventory becomes a recurring challenge, especially when Ukrainian Air Space is still insecure. Radek's role was to improve the logistic supply speed whilst still protecting the security of such stocks and their onward shipment across Ukraine. None of the fifty or more Ramstein Defence Contact Group would be best pleased with Poland if their armament contributions of any type failed to reach the battlefield for any reason.

Ukraine's Defence Ministry in conjunction with the Ukrainian Army had sent teams to be instructed and trained to use the more sophisticated NATO armaments. For speed, with the mounting Russian offensive gaining traction, such trained personnel would also become the trainers on the battlefield as soldiers rotated. Western Partners were finally waking up to the fact that the Ukrainians had to have weapons capable of striking at a distance of three hundred kilometres ie precision artillery and the relevant munitions. Capability to target Russian Military resupply routes and munitions dumps whether in the occupied territories or inside Russian borderlands will ultimately force its army's withdrawal – that is the perceived military wisdom. Its superior numbers in artillery or troops would of course become irrelevant without shells and bullets as Russian Military supply lines are disrupted and ultimately destroyed.

From Radek's perspective, a similar issue threatened where munitions for specific artillery was once more running low. With the one-year anniversary of the full-scale invasion of Ukraine approaching, a renewed Russian counter-offensive was ever so slowly and incrementally gaining territory. Hence, the Ukrainian Army in order to continue fighting effectively needed the supply of such crucial ammunition to meet this mounting threat. This was succinctly put by NATO Secretary General Jens Stoltenberg on Valentine's Day.

'Key capabilities like ammunition, fuel, and spare parts must reach Ukraine before Russia can seize the initiative on the battlefield. Ukraine is firing artillery shells at the rate of ten thousand per day with Russia expending fifty thousand per day or more. The requirement for such munitions by the Ukrainian Army is only set to increase as the Kremlin's fresh offensive gains momentum in the coming weeks if only to defend Ukraine and its battle lines. Even the

93

current rate of Ukraine's ammunition usage is many times higher than NATO's current rate of production while depleting still ever-reducing allied stockpiles. Our Defence Industries are now under increasing strain as waiting times for munitions, particularly large caliber, are unacceptable. The Western military alliance is facing a serious problem of simultaneously supplying Ukraine's growing needs and rebuilding NATO stockpiles.'

Radek recalled Witoria Hanko highlighting this very issue in a recent January meeting with Lieutenant-General Politczek before he left for Mielec. The production capabilities of factories and logistics chains in Western Countries were simply not set up to service a large-scale land war after decades of mostly fighting and servicing smaller-scale wars against poorly-armed insurgencies like in Afghanistan. She had pointed out the United States earlier deliveries of 1600 Stinger surface-to-air missiles and 8500 Javelin anti-tank missiles was the equivalent of 13 and 5 years production respectively for the Defence firm Raytheon Technologies; even partnering with a fellow arms company, Lockheed Martin, has only increased production to 400 Javelin missiles per month. Witoria had stated the reality is the Western Military Defence complex is unprepared for a long war from ammunition to supply logistics to training. NATO needs, she also commented - not just because of the war in Ukraine - a proper Industrial Defence plan to be prepared for any escalations in other parts of the world; whether Russia, China, Iran, North Korea, or others. The shortcomings of the post-Cold War model were now increasingly self-evident.

The West's short term issues of military armaments production and developing an Industrial Defence Plan were of course not Radek's problems to solve. It rested with Politicians, Industrialists, and Military High Commands. His issues were more immediate - fires to be quenched. The daily influx of equipment created inventory and warehousing challenges even for Poland's military. He had quickly sought to minimize material handling by prioritizing the Ukrainian battlefield requests for munitions in particular straight to the railhead spurs. Such items were then directly loaded either into rail wagons or articulated trailers depending on the designated intermediate logistic Ukrainian hubs. Similarly, Leopard II battle tanks were rechecked by Polish Maintenance crews before being loaded onto flatbed wagons, fueled but not armed. The Ukrainian High Command wanted this heavy armour transported as received so brigade strength units could begin to be assembled. Four man tank crews had already been undergoing fast track training on the Leopards for some weeks in Finland, Germany, Poland, and the Baltics. As for the British Challenger battle tanks, these were already in Ukraine with their crews training on Salisbury Plain in the United Kingdom. Whilst the Stryker and Bradley armoured fighting vehicles had also left Poland on flatbeds as part of again the Ukraine's Military Strategists developing plan to form brigade strength mechanized units, Radek was still left with controlling the dispersal warehousing of inventory and overall security protection from any external threats. This included ensuring the war readiness and maintenance of the technologically sophisticated equipment prior to a Ukrainian deployment drawdown.

Protection of the Ukrainian Skies remains the present priority to protect civilians and infrastructure. The Patriot missile system is gradually being provided with the United States, Germany, Netherlands and Poland assisting its deployment. This highly sophisticated system has a range of up to one hundred and fifty kilometres depending on the type of missile used and requires specialised training. It provides excellent air defence against cruise missile types and enemy aircraft. Nevertheless, up to one hundred soldiers are required to operate a Patriot system from the radar to the control station to the missile launcher. Again whilst Ukrainians who will operate this advanced equipment have begun to be trained in the United States at Fort Sill in Oklahoma and Fort Bliss in Texas, Iranian drones in particular are still a challenge for NATO air defence systems as they typically fly low and are hard to detect. In addition, the ammunition to shoot them down can often cost more than the drones themselves raising the costs of warfare. A single Patriot missile costs US$ 3 million making it unsuitable against incoming drones. As Radek watched another batch of German-made Gepard mechanised vehicles to add to the 30 already in Ukraine being loaded onto flatbed wagons, armament that can send dual streams of 35mm rounds ripping into the sky to hit such drones, his face reflected an inner chagrin and grimness. Although the weapon, essentially an anti-aircraft gun, Ukraine has at least the start of a mobile air defence system capable of destroying Russian drones and missiles. The hold-up in shipping more of such equipment related solely to the Swiss-made ammunition. Perhaps German manufacturer Rheinmetall saying a new production line to start making 35mm ammunition or sheer embarrassment politically at the impact of its War Materials Law, the Swiss government had week's earlier revoked non-re-export clauses as a two-thirds majority of the United Nations General Assembly had decided Russia's War in Ukraine had violated International Law – a political escape! Whilst the Gepards would work well against drone swarms, the Ukrainians had not waited for a Western solution and taken the initiative. Jeeps were adapted to field a heavy machine gun together with thermal and night sight imaging plus laser targeting. Stepan had told him about the mobility and success of the adapted jeeps but the supply of the drones had to be stopped at source. Radek wondered whether the recent attack on an industrial centre in Tehran was a forerunner of more decisive action by the Ukrainians or the Israelis. In the interim, mortars of calibre 60 mm and more, grenade launchers – automatic and manual – of calibre 30 and 40 mm, stand-mounted anti-tank grenade launchers, and thermobaric grenade launchers were the bread and butter armaments he saw with munitions heading to those embattled trenches in the Donbas along with more heavy artillery to repel the growing Russian counter-offensive.

For now, Radek and his Polish Military colleagues were entirely focussed on delivering the right armament, in the right quantity, in the right operational condition, at the right time, and to the right designated military destination as identified by the Ukrainian Defence Ministry.

Chapter 20

The cloak of familiarity was very much woven into the Surgeon's disguise. Seeing an amiable Swedish Professor in and around Niepolomice, making a conscious effort to speak Polish over the weeks, merely endeared him to villagers and strangers alike. In the mid-afternoon of St Valentine's Day, Professor Lars Andersson was once more exercising his retrievers on the open land between his rented house and the Król compound. Clearly, his target's recent posting to Poland's Eastern Logistics hub based in and around Mielec was denying him any leave to see his family. However, 'the Surgeon' had guessed correctly that if there was to be any date prior to Easter when his target would appear, it was today. Around 16:00, as daylight was just starting to begin moving towards dusk, a military Mercedes s500 limousine appeared on the single track leading to the compound followed by a Toyota Land cruiser.

Even a meticulous assassin like 'the Surgeon' can enjoy a moment of pure luck of being in the right place at the right time. Returning from walking the retrievers, he found himself by the gate to the compound calling one of the dogs in Swedish. Bearing in mind the dogs had been bred and trained by a Polish breeder, it was no surprise to the Professor his calls were being ignored. For the arriving vehicles, it looked as if yet another pet owner was losing his voice trying to corral uncontrollable animals. For Radek's personal protection officers, they were not so easily swayed. The officer in the front passenger seat of the limousine spoke to his colleagues in the Toyota. In an instant, the Mercedes came to a halt. The Land Cruiser swung by heading at speed towards the Professor with blue warning lights flashing. A confused and bespectacled man with dog leads was suddenly facing two men in suits stepping out from the Toyota. The driver stayed in the vehicle with the engine running whilst the officer in the passenger seat half crouched behind the open passenger door pointing a Glock 19 at his body mass. The other officer, hand gun drawn, shouted 'On the ground now!'

'The Surgeon's' body language in response to guns being pointed at him as a simple Professor was worthy of an Oscar. Dropping the dog leads instantaneously he looked to his left right and then behind him whilst filling his face with a look of complete confusion. Shouts from both officers to get down on the ground were ignored as he responded in Swedish and then repeating with a heavily accented and feigning stuttering 'I do not understand' in Polish. His apparent panic was ignored as the officer approaching from the left threw him, after a stomach punch, brusquely to the ground. However, in role as a man in his mid to late fifties, 'the Surgeon' offered no resistance even when his legs were also kicked apart and his body frisked for any concealed weapon. His cries between gasping for air, in alternating Swedish and Polish of 'What have I done, what am I accused of' resulted in him eventually being dragged to his feet. The Professor was by now covered in mud, grass, and wet even with Swedish Klättermusen outerwear. With the threat level diminishing, the Mercedes Limousine pulled up behind the Toyota. As Radek approached, he saw a man in his late fifties fumbling in his jacket for presumably his wallet to address the demands from his Protection Officers for his identification card or something to establish who he was. 'The Surgeon' was deliberately shaking to simulate fear and innocence as his wallet slipped from his grasp. When it fell open it exposed a Swedish Passport just as the retrievers covered in mud from their walk joined the fray. The Protection Team were not best pleased as the retrievers were jumping up wanting to play and covering their suits in mud and dog hair. One officer checked the details to Niepolomice residents on the Toyota's in-built computer and then handed the passport and Swedish identification card to Radek. The commotion at the gate was seen by Alexandra on the kitchen's close circuit screen and, seeing Radek amongst the melee, headed out after grabbing a winter jacket and pulling on her boots.

By the time she arrived at the gate accompanied by the posse of barking St Bernards, Radek was apologising to the Professor for the rough treatment meted out to him by his bodyguards.

In broken and heavily accented Polish, after initialling speaking a few words of Swedish ... 'You must be a very important man Sir ... to warrant such protection.'

Handing the Professor back his passport and Swedish identity card, Radek was about to reply when Alexandra suddenly appeared next to him.

'Professor, are you alright?' The regular dog walks and seemingly chance meetings in the Town Centre were about to pay off.

'The Surgeon' still feigning shortness of breath and shaking as any innocent person would after the shock of such an encounter was then helped into the limousine by Alexandra. Once inside the house, Alexandra ushered him through the boot room leaving his outerwear and boots to dry by the gas boiler. Yet, as she hung the clothes, the Swedish Klättermusen branding was noted and immediately forgotten by her. As the Professor sat at the kitchen table, his hands shaking just a little for effect prior to cupping them around a large hot mug of tea, Radek reappeared from upstairs after changing into jeans and a rollneck. It was apparent to 'the Surgeon' that Alexandra and Radek were very much in love as they stood arms round one another looking and talking to this bespectacled Swedish Professor, Lars Andersson. He had noted the CCTV system and as dusk fell thermal imaging highlighting the St Bernards when they were not triggering the external lighting. It was time to learn more about the house.

'Mrs Król, I thank you for your most kind hospitality but I really must be going home as my trousers are wet and I need to change into some dry clothes. In addition, I do have to clean my dogs after their afternoon walk.'

This exemplified the Surgeon's depth of thinking as he stalked his quarry. No request to visit the lavatory more a subtle entry into initially the upstairs and then taking advantage of the Króls feelings for each other, he could have time to gain inside knowledge about the house layout.

'Certainly not Professor, let me take you upstairs to a guest bedroom and find a pair of Radek's tracksuit bottoms for you. As for the dogs, they are in the back of the Toyota asleep so you need not worry.'

When Alexandra disappeared into a bedroom and then reappeared with a clean pair of tracksuit bottoms, 'the Surgeon' knew instantly where the master bedroom was. Ushered into a guest bedroom and left to change, his eyes were sweeping the front of the property before leaving to see the rear garden area from another upstairs bedroom. Still in his stocking feet he gingerly came down the stairs clutching his wet trousers knowing that pretending to be disoriented as he wandered about downstairs looking for that elusive gas boiler. A quick glance through the slightly open door into the kitchen so the lovers in an engrossing embrace, he had time. Opening a door off the hall, steps led down into a basement, seeing the light switch, he turned it on and went down. It was racked out with some shelves full of homemade preservatives and others filled with carpentry tools. However what really caught his eye was a steel door in the corner that appeared freshly installed. Before he could investigate further, he heard Alexandra calling out 'Professor' repeatedly. It was time to reappear. Alexandra was half way up the first flight of stairs when 'the Surgeon' responded from the hall 'my apologies Mrs Król but I cannot find the boiler room'.

Chapter 21

Karel Veselý was a discreet man. In the clandestine market in which he operated, names were never mentioned even his. Transactions were simple. A list of requirements from the Client followed by a quote with a 100% provided in either US dollars or euros. His reputation as an armourer was second to none as whatever weapons and munitions were requested, the items were always brand new from the relevant manufacturer with the identification numbers removed as necessary. His legitimate base of operation was a small backstreet garage with space for four or five cars if two were on the hydraulic ramps over the inspection pits. Appointments were made through the dark net usually in coffee shops with an intermediary handling the transaction. Karel was extremely careful and would have the potential client watched before transacting any business. Apart from ensuring the Client was not in fact working for any Government body from the Police to Secret Services, the armourer's precautions had even protected two clients by highlighting they were under surveillance.

'The Surgeon' was aware that his list of requirements was likely to cause even Karel Veselý to question who he was. Similarly, Veselý would probably link his weapons and munitions supply to the eventual assassination of his target over the Easter Weekend. What identity did he assume to conduct the transaction? Clearly the Professor, Hans Fischer, and of course Peter van de Berg were non-starters.

Liberica Cafe on Valentinska in Prague's Old Town was the designated meeting point. Tommaso Genovese was sat in a corner with clear lines of sight to the entrance, kitchen, and lavatories with a half drunk double espresso in front of him and Dolce & Gabbana sunglasses similarly resting on the table. Vesely's intermediary entered the coffee shop and spotted his boss's client. The jet black greased hair, close cropped black beard, grey toothed jacket, black cashmere rollneck, black belt, trousers and shoes, and stylish silver Ferragamo belt buckle – 'the Surgeon' looked every inch of being related to the Genovese Family and its criminal wealth. The intermediary sat down in front of 'the Surgeon' feeling strangely uneasy with hairs on the back of his neck suddenly raised. A folded paper listing the weapons required but handwritten was pushed to the middle of the table. As the intermediary went to pull it towards himself, he found himself looking at a stiletto between his middle fingers and pinning the folded paper to the table. A bubble of blood appeared from one of his fingers.

'Silenzio' was the word uttered by 'the Surgeon' with such underlying menace that the intermediary picked up the folded paper and seemingly ran rather than walked from the coffee shop. There was no handshake, no offer of a coffee, and no small talk atall.

Karel Vesely read the weapons list with euros on his mind rather than any damage such armaments would inflict. His intermediary had relayed what had transpired a few

104

hours earlier in the Liberica Café. The message from the Genovese was clear – there was to be no speculation or careless talk about what this weaponry would or could be used for either before or after the transaction was completed; and especially subsequently if it became public knowledge.

'The Surgeon' had considered on taking delivery of the armaments executing Veselý, the intermediary, or indeed anyone else that might lead the authorities to his role in fulfilling the contract. However, dealing with the bodies assuming he had even managed to eradicate every tenuous link was too dangerous for a man who was a ghost and working alone. The better alternative was to utilise the soft but threatening power of an Italian Mafia Family. Something even Veselý would respect if he wanted to avoid looking over his shoulder for the rest of, what would be, a short Life. This had led to his choice of name, wardrobe, and physical look. It was a masterclass in make-up as 'the Surgeon' used black hair dye to change his naturally blonde hair and now trimmed beard so much in evidence in his role as the Professor in Niepolomice. Tommaso Genovese's swarthy appearance and his use of a skin tone to move his face and hands towards a light dark to olive mediterranean hue - a Mafiosi and made-man.

A week later Karel Veselý entered the Liberica Café and recognised Tommaso Genovese instantly, from the description of his intermediary, sitting once again in the corner of the café. A slim black leather briefcase was pushed gently along the floor towards Veselý by Tommaso's feet. 'The Surgeon' had carefully filled the case wearing nitrile kitchen gloves and then wiped the handle for prints carrying it to the meeting wearing leather gloves. Veselý wisely decided not to open the briefcase as to do so in the café would be treated as an insult by any member of the Genovese Clan. An address in a Soviet era industrial estate in eastern Prague was to be the handover point for the armaments. However before passing a note with this address, Veselý wished to assure his client that the Mafia's code of silence, omertà, would be strictly followed. His reasoning was personal as he had a wife and three young children that he adored hence Veselý had broken his own protocol of never meeting a client. The weaponry requested, though obtained, scared him and the description of Tommaso Genovese by his intermediary had unnerved him. Looking across the table, Veselý watched as the man opposite removed his sunglasses to reveal deep brown, almost black, coloured eyes. They were empty and emotionless sending an involuntary shiver down his back. He attempted to speak but the man raised a single finger to his lips. There was to be no conversation. Veselý had wanted to assure his client that each item on the list had been separately sourced as if for multiple clients not just one. This action was as much to protect him as the Genovese. Putting on his sunglasses, death left the café.

Chapter 22

The February Annual Munich Security Conference was swiftly followed by President Joe Biden's unannounced visit to Kyiv. The timing was immediately and deliberately prior to the first anniversary of Russia's wholesale invasion of Ukraine. Radek was ordered to be part of ABW's security detail whilst the United States President was on Polish soil. This meant leaving Mielec for Przemysl to meet the President's returning train from Kyiv. Radek was then in charge of escorting him safely to Rzeszow Airfield. Air Force One was already waiting to fly the President to Warsaw for the start of his three day official visit to Poland.

Radek was pleased to see Air Force One and its precious cargo safely in the air so he could return to Mielec. The armament shipments were increasing daily as more weapons and munitions made their way East. Breaking for a late lunch, TVN channel was showing the meeting between the United States and Polish Presidents. The true story of Biden's meeting with Pope John Paul II when a Senator made Radek and other serving soldiers in Mielec's canteen stand cheering with pride in their hearts to be a Pole. There was also great admiration for Biden's bravery in visiting Kyiv. Travelling by night train through a warzone without the customary protections of a United States President, and as

Leader of the Free World, Biden sent a message of American Courage and steadfastness in this fight for democracy. As for the Ukrainian people after suffering the indiscriminate destruction of homes and infrastructure, there was now more than just hope in every heart. The inevitability of Ukraine's victory with its territorial integrity restored permanently was now in embodied in Ukraine's will to repulse the Russian invaders. Radek also now strongly believed, seeing at first hand the increasing volume of modern precision armaments passing through Mielec, defeat of the 2nd largest army in the world was becoming the art of the possible.

Relaxing in the Mielec Officers Mess with a bottle of Belvedere Vodka for company, TVN's Breaking News on February 21st was focused on President Putin's speech. The newscaster pointed out the audience in the Kremlin was handpicked, Regional Governors, Senior Military Officers, and Secret Service personnel. Nevertheless, its content was directed not only at the ordinary Russian but also those in the Global community. Sadly, both groups swallowed unbelievably the Kremlin's propaganda. For the West, there was nothing new or credible in Russia's inexcusable reasoning for the use of force. It was certainly not in response to NATO aggression as Radek knew downing another shot of vodka. This false narrative implying Russia is the victim of the West's actions he thought defies reality. In 2014, Crimea was occupied by the Russian Army crossing internationally recognised borders of Ukraine in breach of the United Nations Charter. Territorial integrity cannot be changed by force; without forgetting the Kremlin had also coerced, fermented, and financed rebellion in the Luhansk and Donetsk Oblasts adding to the subversion of an independent and free Ukrainian State. Sadly how an autocracy, Radek pondered, still controlled the perception of the Kremlin's activities as morally right defied belief? Warping the facts to a pliant population across eleven time zones was hardly going to undergo the scrutiny of a free and active media let alone active opposition debate in the Duma. The United States National Security Adviser summed up the implausibility of Putin's justification for the war with the words - *'there is a kind of absurdity in the notion that Russia was under some form of military threat from Ukraine or anyone else'*.

As the evening wore on with clips of the United States President being welcomed by President Andrzej Duda, attention turned on the newscast to Biden's contrasting fiery speech from Warsaw's Royal Palace. He made it clear the United States would not waver even as the conflict enters a new and more uncertain phase. Western resolve was, in his words, stiffening in the face of Putin's assault on democracy and freedom. Autocrats only understand one word – No, you will not take my country. No, you will not take my freedom. No, you will not take my future; also Biden did not hold back from pointedly accusing Putin of atrocities and war crimes. The Kremlin's unprovoked attack was nothing short of an expansionist and imperialist Russia's craven lust for land thereby dismissing outright the West started the war.

Another busy day in Mielec with German tanks, spares, and munitions arriving left Radek exhausted as he slumped into a comfy armchair in his officer's billet. The repetitive jingle of TVN's nightly Breaking News broadcast woke him up from a deep sleep. The newscast was reporting the meeting of the leaders of the 'Bucharest 9' *(the countries on NATO's eastern flank and former Warsaw Pact Members from the Soviet era formed on Putin's annexation of Crimea in 2014)* on February 22nd in Warsaw. Whilst hosted by the Polish President, as the war in continues, the Bucharest 9 anxieties have remained heightened unless the Ukrainian Military delivers a decisive victory regaining all occupied territory. Whilst Biden stated the obvious that the Eastern Flank was the frontline of NATO's collective defence, the freedom of democracies throughout Europe and around the world was what was really at stake under the United Nations Rules based Order.

NATO Secretary General Jens Stoltenberg, who was attending the meeting, said *'We do not know when the war will end, but when it does, we need to ensure that history does not repeat itself. We cannot allow Russia to continue to chip away at European security. We must break the cycle of Russian aggression.'* Biden closed reiterating that *'NATO's mutual-defence pact, Article 5, is sacred. The United States and you will defend together literally every inch of NATO territory'* having earlier praised the eastern flank countries for their efforts in taking in Ukrainian refugees with giving particular attention to Poland's efforts.

The newscast anchor then switched to a rally held hours earlier in the Luzhniki Stadium in Moscow. Speaking at this state-organized concert before the national holiday for 'Defender of the Fatherland Day' on February 23rd, Putin delivered a notably short address, less than five minutes, to a seemingly capacity crowd of possibly around one hundred thousand. The Polish newscaster reported that according to the Russian Police double that amount of Russian Patriots had attended the free concert. This made Radek laugh as the newscaster reminded the Polish television audience that the Luzhniki Stadium had a seating capacity of eighty one thousand. Again, for there to be a large crowd, attendance at such official rallies was manipulated for the State's propaganda purposes. The majority of the crowd was made up of employees of state-run companies and government agencies, who had been told by their superiors to attend. Organizers of the event had apparently promised to distribute Russian flags to all attendees and additionally, according to the newscaster, hot meals as the temperature was already in double figures below zero this week. Radek was left asking himself 'If only'. 'If only' the Russians had a free press. When Putin mentioned that Russia was fighting for its historical lands, Radek almost broke the remote. However, the President's speech was preceded apparently by performances from pro-war artists, Russian military veterans, and a group of Ukrainian children apparently from the city of Mariupol. As the Polish commentator highlighted, Mariupol was devastated in the early months of the invasion by attritional and scorched earth tactics by the Russian Army. The use of Ukrainian children separated from family and loved ones for propaganda purposes made Radek sick to the stomach. The newscaster highlighted Russia had been accused of forcibly deporting thousands of Ukrainian children to Russian territory and putting them up for adoption. Thus, this manipulation of these children in the Luzhniki Stadium struck Radek as constituting yet another distasteful and heinous war crime as he fell asleep.

Lieutenant-General Politczek had decided to visit Mielec. He had, without thinking, missed Radek's attendance and input at his regular Friday meetings with his senior team.

However, with the volume of armaments now being delivered into Eastern Poland, it was an overdue priority to see first-hand just what the impact of this daily and nightly armament tsunami of deliveries was having on Poland's military inventory controls and speed of shipments to Ukraine's battlefront. Against this background, Grzegorz accompanied by Colonels Chmura and Hanko landed mid-morning at Mielec Military Airbase. Radek met them as they left the comfort of the Dassault Falcon 900 and began a tour of the many depots around the new railheads.

After lunch at Mielec's Officers Mess, they all adjourned to a private room for ABW's Friday Meeting. Radek was the first to speak.

'Whilst I await, with much interest, to learn General what decisions were made at the meeting of the Bucharest 9, the continued official absence of Finland and Sweden from such discussions impacts our security whatever decisions might have been taken. In my view the rationale behind the current Russian offensive is to disrupt Ukraine's ability to regenerate sufficient capacity for its counteroffensive. Hence the open questions are how badly Ukraine's casualty rates have gone up in stopping that Russian offensive and the current state of its military reserves? Thus, as we all know, it is now a race against time for the advanced heavy armaments and precision weaponry pledged by the West to reach the battlefront - if Ukraine is ever to reclaim occupied areas this year. Our Prime Minister, Mateusz Morawiecki, is in Kyiv today marking one year since the beginning of Russia's invasion as four Polish Leopard 24A tanks with their trained crews are delivered to Ukraine's Military. As you saw today, the remaining ten with crews will leave Poland within the following twelve days. Germany has pledged to send eighty eight Leopard 1 tanks to Ukraine and in addition a further fourteen state-of-the-art Leopard 2A6 tanks have already arrived here in Poland for shipment. The Spanish, ten, and Finnish, three, Leopards are expected to be delivered by air into Mielec over this weekend. Whilst other countries pledged Leopard 2 tanks are expected within the next two weeks (including the Germany's promised Leopard 1s), Rheinmetall and Krauss-Maffei Wegmann, two German companies that produce the Leopard tanks jointly, are working with our and Ukraine's maintenance units to establish an effective repair and spares system close to the battlefield frontlines. In the interim, Ukraine's defenders are hoping to inflict as much pain on the Russians as possible while preparing for their own counteroffensive. Kyiv's spring attack might well, I believe, focus on the southern front, seeking to cut Russia's land access to Crimea together with destroying the Kerch Bridge wholesale as precision missiles take out military targets. The establishment of at least two tank regiments of seventy two or more tanks will punch through the Russian lines with combined air, artillery, and mechanised infantry. I hope NATO is following the British lead and already training pilots.'

'General, I am concerned that Finland and Sweden are not yet already full NATO members let alone not even direct parties to any Bucharest 9 discussions. The Swedish Intelligence Service (SÄPO) has stated publicly that Russia is the single biggest threat to Sweden's security. My contact in Stockholm tells me that Russia's aggressive and extremist actions through its hybrid activities pose the most serious threat since the Cold War. From cyber-attacks to poisoning social media to infiltrating with funding society's disruptive and dissident groups is a Russian attempt to build up an ability to create an entirely alternative social and power structure. Whilst these are broad and complex risks all Western countries face with such destabilising activities by Russia's FSB, the Baltic, Belarus, and the Suwalki corridor are all matters of increasing importance to the Bucharest 9 and the Nordic countries plus Germany.

Following Russia's further invasion of Ukraine, Sweden, along with neighbouring Finland, broke with its decades-long policy of military non-alignment and declared themselves as candidates for NATO membership. Yet here we are ten months later with Sweden's application still opposed in particular by Turkey. The accession protocols of new NATO members must be ratified by all thirty members of the organization. Only Hungary and Turkey have not yet had their parliaments ratify the agreement for the accession of the two Nordic countries. Hungarian Prime Minister, Viktor Orban, stated earlier today that Hungary supports Finland and Sweden's NATO membership. Nevertheless, Turkey's concerns, who, he noted, are also our Allies, regarding Sweden's entry should be heard if the expansion effort is to succeed. Turkey has recently indicated its immediate approval of only Finland for NATO membership. As for Hungary, its Parliament has been delayed by a flurry of legislation required to unlock European Union funds but next week the accession of the Nordic Countries is to be debated. However, Orban and his FIDESZ party machine have, in my opinion and that of my team, been working for the last twelve months to undermine support for the European Union, NATO, and indeed Ukraine whilst brainwashing the Hungarian public into supporting Russia. It is a political charade aimed at enhancing the optics for various stakeholders, including Russia, Hungary's key energy supplier, Turkey, and the electorate. Orban's manoeuvres are laughable but are being used to delay ratification. His somewhat contradictory statements mask inaction. Why say being a NATO member was vital for Hungary yet in the same breath his government would not send arms to Ukraine? Maintaining its economic ties with Moscow while lobbying hard against any European Union sanctions? Again, after being dominated by Moscow for decades before the collapse of communism, Orban reiterated Hungary had a moral obligation in principle to support the bid of the Nordic countries in spite of incurring geopolitical issues like Finland's 1000 kilometre border with Russia. Why this latter caveat if not providing cover for his Government's inaction?

Turkish ratification of the Finnish and Swedish bids depends on how quickly Stockholm fulfils the counter-terrorism promises made in Madrid last year with Ankara. Sweden is, I understand, fully committed to implementing the agreement but some six more months may well be required to write and pass the new laws. This will then allow the Swedish judicial system to implement the new definitions of terrorism. Sweden, from the Turkish viewpoint, will then no longer be a safe haven for Kurdish militants, particularly those of the Kurdistan Workers' Party (PKK). Such people, who Ankara blamed for the 2016 attempted coup, will no longer be able to collect money, recruit members, and engage in other nefarious activities. It will send a very clear message to the PKK and others that Sweden is not a safe place for terrorists. The Turkish parliament would intend to ratify Ankara's decision on the two Nordic countries' membership at the same time rather than separately. However, Turkish presidential and parliamentary elections are expected this May with Turkey's parliament going into recess some time before the elections. Hence, unless pressure can be brought to bear, I can see this slipping into the second half of this year contrary to all our security interests along NATO's Eastern Flank. NATO Secretary-General Jens Stoltenberg has met with Turkey's Foreign Minister, Mevlüt Çavuşoğlu, this week in Istanbul stating Nordic Membership should be ratified as soon as possible whether together or separately; adding his voice to that of Germany's Foreign Minister, Annalena Baerbock, calling on Turkey and Hungary to allow Finland and Sweden to join NATO without further delay.'

'Thanks Jan, perhaps I can ease Radek's and your concerns, maybe also Witoria's, after we have heard from her. Witoria'

'I would like to remind us of President Biden's statements this week - *... we have to be honest and clear-eyed as we look at the year ahead. The defence of freedom is not the work of a day. It is always difficult and it is always important ...* and ... *the truth of the matter is - the United States needs Poland and NATO as much as NATO needs the United States.* Gentlemen, there will be no let-up in Russia's Imperialist attempt to seize more territory in Ukraine. Yet the surprising resilience of the Ukrainian people and the unexpected ineptitude of the Russian forces have prevented a full takeover. Instead, the war has become what NATO's Secretary General and others have described as a grinding war of attrition without a discernible end. The West has been shipping tranches of arms, equipment, ammunition, and now tanks to Ukraine on a steadily increasing level for the last twelve months. However, the absence of offensive weaponry has meant the trajectory of the war and battlefield has broadly been a stalemate. Only in this New Year has the West finally realised how stupid it has been to fear any threats made by the Kremlin. As the late President Roosevelt said in his speech after the Japanese attack on Pearl Harbour ... *the only thing we need to fear is fear itself.*

Threats of nuclear armageddon after China and India have made their views very clear and public, are simply empty and toothless. As we have seen today the area around Mielec has become the equivalent of a massive Amazon logistics hub shipping weapons *'in and out'*. Can this amazing influx of weaponry to Ukraine from armoured mechanised vehicles, longer-range missiles and artillery, and together with Patriot and other air defence systems make Ukraine prevail on the battlefield? We have all agreed today and previously that Zelensky needs to win rather than be provided with just enough to survive. Tanks are arriving at long last and crews are now being trained yet the Ukrainians need to be supplied with everything possible to win including F16s. Time is not on Zelensky's or Ukraine's side to win and then have a strong negotiating position to end to the war? Concerns about supplies of ammunition and weapons have emerged in the past week. The West cannot provide clearly unlimited support forever as the arms industries' production is struggling to adjust to the heightened consumption and the ability also simultaneously to restock NATO inventories. Similarly, political and electorate support for the war effort will start to wane if this war moves into 2024 without any prospect of an end. This is of course why Putin believes that Russia can outlast Ukraine's resistance, especially if a future change in the White House heralded a shift in policy towards Ukraine. Putin has made it very clear that he is prepared to sacrifice whatever it takes and that is part of the problem. There are lots of statements being made and rumours coming out of the Kremlin that Putin is willing to see last year's mobilisation of three hundred thousand people slaughtered on the battlefield let alone a further half million likely to be called up this June.

Ukraine must now strike legitimate targets inside Russia and occupied Crimea to win this war. You cannot win this fight if you do not hit your enemy. Ukrainian forces should target every military base from airfields to missile bases to missile launchers to military logistic warehouses ie any military facility is fair game. These are legitimate targets and must be destroyed. I believe that this will happen and Ukraine will drive Russia's army from all occupied territory, including Crimea. So when Putin's war of choice fails, will the inner circle harden its repressive controls even more to keep order across the country or will chaos rule in Russia which has of course the largest stockpile of nuclear warheads in the world. Either way nothing good can be expected. There will be too many destabilising factors from a tanking economy as Western Sanctions finally bite to separatist and breakaway sentiments coming to the fore in the regions. Will the inner circle stick with Putin as the only apparent person who can keep control and thus protect the wealth they have corruptly plundered over the last two decades? Will the regions as federal budgets and subsidies are reduced, question why they need Moscow? Will there be an attempt to install an alternative figure to keep the situation under control or on the other hand, with the power to start long overdue reforms? The worst outcome would be if Ukraine is unable to take back most of the remaining occupied territory before the end of this year. By that time, a new wave of Russian-trained forces and Russian manufactured military equipment will start to become available to Russia's High Command. At that point, a long-term stalemate could well be in prospect.

When Russia invaded Ukraine a year ago, the Kremlin wanted to create a land corridor through southern Ukraine to the Moscow-backed breakaway region of Transnistria; a narrow strip of land almost two hundred kilometres long and thirty kilometres wide between the Dniester River and Moldova's eastern border with Ukraine. Transnistria is not recognised as a sovereign state by the international community or, indeed, even by Russia, although since 1992 just under two thousand Russian soldiers, classified amazingly as peacekeepers, have been stationed there. In recent days, Putin has once again revived his imperialistic narrative that Russia is fighting for historic frontiers and borders. A concept already used in attempts to justify the Ukraine invasion and could of course be used to justify aggression against almost any of Russia's neighbours, as well as Moldova. Russian Imperialism must be constrained by a full-on diplomatic effort to complement success on the battlefield. I was heartened by the United Nations General Assembly in New York overwhelmingly backing a resolution condemning Russia's invasion of Ukraine of a year ago. The motion was supported by one hundred and forty one nations with thirty two abstaining and seven - including Russia - voting against. The resolution reaffirmed support for Ukraine's sovereignty and territorial integrity, rejecting any Russian claims to the parts of the country it occupies. It demanded the Russian Federation immediately, completely and unconditionally withdraws all of its military forces from the territory of Ukraine back within its internationally recognized borders and also called for a cessation of hostilities. Whilst the resolution was passed overwhelmingly by the majority of nations, there were some notable abstentions namely China, India, Iran and South Africa. As for the seven countries who voted against along with Russia, were Belarus, North Korea, Eritrea, Mali, Nicaragua and Syria, hardly a surprise? The measure is not legally binding but does hold political weight.

The reaction to Russia sending a delegation this week to the Organization for Security and Co-operation in Europe (OSCE) provides some hope that Russia's pariah status is becoming paramount within the diplomatic community. The OSCE was of course founded in 1975 to improve relations between the Western and Eastern blocs with its current members including members of NATO and allies of Russia. In Vienna, a large number of delegates walked out during a Russian address at a parliamentary session of the European security body. This walkout and the United Nations vote happened yesterday before the first anniversary of the invasion. The Austrian government rather lamely stated it was obliged to grant visas under international law because the OSCE had its headquarters in Vienna. Ukraine and Lithuania boycotted the session entirely over Austria's decision to invite officials from Moscow despite some if not all being under European Union sanctions. Latvian Member of Parliament, Rihards Kols, said out loud in that opening session what should have been obvious. The Russian delegation were war criminals and sanctioned individuals yet people were supposed to sit in the chamber and say nothing. General, we need much more calling out of Russia's unacceptable presence and continued infiltration of Institutions until the Kremlin drops once and for all its imperialist ambitions.'

'Witoria, am I correct that Pan Kols quoted the Ukrainian Border Guards on Snake Island's message to the Moskva on February 25th 2022?

'Yes General – to that Russian Warship – *Go f**k yourself!*'

'Is there anything else, we should be thinking about Witoria?'

'Putin revoked a decree this week that had committed Russia to a settlement in Transnistria respecting Moldova's territorial integrity. This does not indicate an immediate attack on Moldova as Russia currently lacks the military capability. Nevertheless, it does point towards an escalation in Russia's ongoing efforts to undermine the Moldovan state. Moldova's President Maia Sandu earlier this month highlighted intelligence suggesting Russia was plotting to overthrow the Moldovan authorities and sow chaos in the small former Soviet republic. Hence, Russia's Defence Ministry accusation that Ukraine was planning to invade Moldova's breakaway Transnistria region. Using a false-flag operation purportedly by Russian forces as the pretext for such an invasion alerts me to how Russia continues to accuse others of such acts before actually doing so themselves. Therefore, even though Moldova is neither in NATO nor a member of the European Union, we need to be more than ready to actively support this economically poor country's democratic freedom and the financial burden it faces with the influx of Ukrainian refugees.'

'I sense these understandable concerns that remedying two decades of the West's ambivalence to Putin's

Russia is taking far too long. However, in unity of response there is great strength but I share your frustrations. NATO will though be enlarging its existing eight multi-national battlegroups from battalion to immediately brigade size. The enhanced forward presence combat ready groups at the Orzysz and Rukla bases will be expanded incorporating air cavalry and specific ground attack fighter aircraft. The Bucharest 9 will by the end of 2023 have a complete Patriot Air Defence network from Estonia to Romania. In addition, the land border defences will be strengthened, including Finland's and Sweden's, with a comprehensive Patriot air defence system across Scandinavia during 2024. Within the NATO air defence package, there will be an unquantified number of German-made Gepard mechanised vehicles to deal with swarms of kamikaze or other attack drones together with other available equipment to counter any drone threat. With the Finnish and Swedish accession, the Baltic becomes in effect a NATO sea. These members will meet and agree a formal plan for the naval protection of the coastlines by September. As for Moldova, Biden and the other leaders met President Sandu and agreed to form a Rapid Deployment Force within Romania together with a humanitarian funding package. I concur with your thoughts that Russia's manipulation of Institutions for its own self-serving ends has to stop, particularly its membership of the United Nations Security Council and the shameful use of the veto in total conflict with the spirit of the United Nations Charter. I have no immediate answer but self-serving vetoes have no place in a Rules based Order. Yes legitimate military targets in Russia's borderlands to Ukraine have to happen and be at the mercy of the longer range precision missiles and artillery supplied. Zelensky is only echoing Churchill to Roosevelt – *Give us the tools and we will finish the job.*

Ukrainian pilots, in addition to being in the United Kingdom, are now training on French Dassault Mirages together with Polish and German F16s. I agree that we have to consider Belarus today as Russia so both as NATO's Eastern Flank and entry in Schengen it must be secure. After the OCSE meeting, the European Union countries must properly and really vet any Russian visa request and reflect, with the brutality and butchery in Ukraine, is any such person welcome into our house. Our President is seemingly fixated on the dangers presented by the Suwalki Gap, Jan do you have thoughts given your attachment to NATO's military command last summer? However before you answer let's have a comfort break for five minutes and Radek please organise some fresh tea – considering all these matters is making me thirsty.'

With fresh tea served and everyone once again settled in leather armchairs, Jan began to answer Grzegorz's question.

'General, NATO revised its battle plans for dealing with Kaliningrad in 2014 following Russia's initial invasion. It has been revised and updated since then by military planners this autumn. Russia's Baltic fleet comprises of approximately twenty five thousand naval personnel dispersed over forty surface warships that include amphibious, mine warfare, support tenders and auxiliaries plus seven submarines with two still deployed, as far as I know, in the Mediterranean. Somewhat smaller than the name Fleet might imply. The majority of the ships do of course date from the Soviet era. Its role has been defensive with shore-based anti-ship and air defence capabilities being more of the focus. Nevertheless, Putin did state last summer the intention to modernise the neglected Baltic Fleet with new Admiral Gorshkov frigates capable of firing both cruise and zircon *(hypersonic)* missiles. NATO's concerns in the past, and probably still, have revolved around the probable nuclear missile warheads stored in Kaliningrad. As for the Suwalki corridor, the terrain is complex with substantial forested and undulating areas making ideal ground to trap and destroy advancing Russian armour from Belarus. More importantly, with Finland's and Sweden's accession into NATO, what strategic advantage would a mechanised thrust linking Kaliningrad to Belarus provide except to raise the body count? Bearing in mind the proposed further strengthening proposed in Poland and along the Baltic States, such an intrusion would seem foolhardy.'

'Yes Radek?'

'My contact in Ukrainian Intelligence, Colonel Stepan Nalyvaichenko, who briefed me on Ukrainian Partisan activity, has just sent me an email. With your permission, I would like to read it out?'

Grzegorz nodded signalling Radek should do so.

'Unconfirmed explosions at the Machulishchy air base near Minsk
Belarussian Partisans have carried out a drone attack disabling a Beriev A-50U surveillance aircraft. This Russian AWACS equivalent has airborne command and control capabilities and can track up to sixty targets at a time. Its long-range radar detection system has been used to pinpoint bombing targets in Ukraine. The plane arrived in Belarus on January 3rd and has made more than a dozen sorties linked to

attacks on my country in conjunction with MiG-31K fighter jets already based at Machulishchy airfield. Drones were used by these Partisans but we are awaiting confirmation as to extent of the damage. However, the entire area around the base is now cordoned off with all vehicles and people being searched. Since the start of Russia's invasion a year ago, there have been several acts of unreported sabotage on the rail system in Belarus and Russian regions bordering Ukraine. These attacks are credited to the Belarussian Partisans and Russian anti-war groups respectively. The A-50U is designed to detect, track and identify aerial and large ground and naval targets, transmit data to command posts, and direct fighter jets to aerial targets. Stepan'

'Radek, do you think this indicates wider internal disruption within Belarus?'

'No Jan, Lukashenko has as tight a grip on the populace as Putin does in Russia. All the opposition leaders are either in penal colonies or have left the country. In addition, all those thousands objecting so openly to Lukashenko's fraudulent re-election as President in 2020 are in prison with many still awaiting trial dates. That said, the mood in Belarus is finely balanced which accounts for Lukashenko's hesitancy in becoming more involved in Putin's war. In the medium term, Belarus will, especially if Putin is still ruling Russia, become part of the Russian State ...'

'No doubt under the argument of historical lands!'

Witoria's comment brought some well needed laughter relieving what was a heavy conversation. Radek continued …

 ' … history suggests that any new or future attack on Ukraine from the north, through the Pripet Marshes, would most likely only compound what has been a disaster for the Russian Military. Any transit, whether or not Belarus is totally part of imperialist Russia, through this region would necessarily be restricted to well-known roads, making it much easier for Ukrainian artillery and drones to target the invaders. Thus, any foolhardy attack on Ukraine through the Pripet Marshes today would only hasten Russia's total defeat. You may recall that in late 2021 I led an undercover mission of GROM Team 6 across the Pripiat-Stokhid National Park. The Pripet Marshes are a natural region and vast complex of wetlands and peatlands extending in a belt from Poland to Russia across northern Ukraine and southern Belarus occupying an estimated 270,000 square kilometres. Wetlands and peatlands are notoriously difficult to navigate and cross for both man and machine. The magnitude of the challenge is found to my surprise in an old Polish book entitled *the Mires of the Pripet Region*. The book highlights the strategic significance of the Pripet Marshes and why traversing across this region is so difficult. Large parts of the landscape are marshlands which, by definition, are mainly shallow bodies of open water and waterlogged; a nightmare for military vehicles like tanks weighing over fifty tons and other overweight military vehicles. Secondly, the vast peatland areas might appear from the surface to be drier as they typically lack open areas of surface water. Peat is approximately ninety per cent by weight water and thus has almost no bearing strength. Thirdly, large tracts of Pripiat consist of swamps, forested wetlands, and peatlands makes vehicular traffic more than challenging. Navigating such terrain has added difficulties as the land changes according to weather, season, and geographic location. This can make the ground almost impassable and with few inhabited places. Additionally, lines of communication running east and west are extremely rare. The majority of roads and trails have no more than local significance as connections between small villages and hamlets which depending on the season can prove completely useless. I and GROM Team 6 were there in deep winter with regular snowfall and temperatures well below zero. We had shelter but for an invading army of mechanized equipment and infantry it is a non-starter. Hence the threat from Belarus is from missiles. The suggestion of Ukraine's High Command having to deploy major resources with such a natural barrier does not stack up in my view.'

'General, the threat of Russian missile strikes on Ukraine still remains very high until an inter-linked comprehensive air defence system is in place. The priority is to protect its citizens from the indiscriminate or maybe deliberate missile and bomb attacks. However, control of the airspace so the West will deliver fighters is more vital than just training pilots on F16s or Mirages or whatever. Nevertheless, Russia's Black Sea fleet still has five missile carriers with up to thirty two Kalibr missiles each and submarines. I believe the Ukraine's spring counter offensive will encompass crippling the Black Sea Fleet's effectiveness as part of its campaign that will undoubtedly raise the political pressure in the Kremlin.'

'Jan, you have made an important point regarding the Black Sea fleet and the impact of it being neutralised will have. The loss of life alone would change attitudes in the Kremlin about coming to the peace negotiating table. In the past I have talked about the Russian's being chess players and whether dealing with political or military issues, we all need also to be thinking six or more moves ahead. Something all the West's politicians, diplomats, and military have to embrace more – the consequences and ramifications when dealing with this Kremlin Regime that is bereft of any morality. Russia's invasion has forced the West, and in particular NATO, to debate the reality of its lack of military readiness. The post-Cold War peace dividend of lower military spending combined with the inevitable further degrading of armed forces by Governments' yearly reducing expenditure. How do we reconcile that Russia is shooting more artillery rounds a day than Europe is manufacturing in a month? This has belatedly set alarm bells ringing everywhere. The Western instinct, not shared by the Bucharest 9, has been to de-escalate which has been interpreted by the Kremlin to escalate. Correcting mistakes of the past needs common resolve as to strategy and understanding of what to do with Russia – a corrupt and terrorist state. People in the West have to be prepared to fight for democracy and freedom as part of thinking about our defence readiness and ability to mobilize. Anyone with access to a television screen or social media is now well aware just how barbaric and cruel the Kremlin is; an autocracy in pursuit of its goals demonstrating how disposable their people are with its total ambivalence for human life.

The narrative of the war to date is dominated by this Russian brutality and the humiliation of its invasion strategy. The failure to take Kyiv, the sudden collapse in Kharkiv, and the retreat from Kherson all paint a picture of a rotten empire hollowed out to the point of obsolescence by decades of corruption and mismanagement. We need to build on this reality with better public communication on the threats Russia poses with its revanchist imperialism. Our people here in Poland should be better informed as to how Polish Defence capabilities are being improved, along with how these are integrated with our Baltic and Nordic neighbours. The same readiness must take hold among national and NATO decision makers as we resist future Russian sabre rattling. Every country's defence planning objectives, accepting the umbrella of NATO's integrated and overriding strategy, should be broadly able to repel any Russian force from its immediate equipment and inventory. Like Witoria, I am a bit worried about what will happen once the fighting stops. Putting aside the consistent and numerous public statements by Western Politicians - such as *when to negotiate with the Russians for peace is for Ukraine to decide.* Is the end point of the war when Ukraine liberates all the occupied territories? Is this realistic? My perspective is very clear. There will be no lasting solution to the conflict unless all of the territories are liberated. We must not fall for Russia's propaganda or threats. Ukraine is not part of Russia's mythical sphere of influence! Polish and other Bucharest 9 governments must not allow other partners and allies to weaken the West's resolve if there is to be going to be lasting peace across Europe and Ukraine. Generational peace has a high price tag. If we want to have a peace in Europe for generations, all politicians must stay on message that Russian aggression against Ukraine must be met with victory on the battlefield. Russian defeat must be total and final. The Western Alliance must, I fully agree, first supply everything Ukraine asks for and, secondly, build a very strong military deterrence in NATO, especially along NATO's Eastern Flank, the Baltic and Nordic countries, and the Baltic Sea. Creeping complacency in the West that Russia's military poses no conventional threat to NATO is very dangerous. We all know that you should never underestimate the Russians and the Kremlin's willingness to sacrifice millions of people's lives. Russia has not yet been defeated strategically and therefore will pose an existential threat to NATO, and thus Poland, for years.

Whether Putin was or was not an excellent judo athlete, the philosophy is important in understanding how his thinking has probably been influenced from such activities. In any competition bout, one looks for weaknesses in your opponent to throw them off balance. In his dealings with the West, this has been very much Putin's style in his efforts to destabilise NATO and the European Union. Indirect financial funding - of minority political groupings together with fake social media accounts promoting conspiracy theories - are all part of the Kremlin's hybrid warfare to distract Governments. I am concerned by United States intelligence sources suggesting that drones and ammunition shipments for Russia's war effort against Ukraine are under consideration by Beijing. Tensions are already high and if that line was crossed, I can envisage international trade and globalisation of production being severely disrupted if not halted to say the least.'

'Understood General but let's not forget China did abstain in the United Nations recent vote condemning Russia's invasion of Ukraine. Furthermore, in its recent Peace Proposal, it acknowledged the importance of territorial integrity and sovereignty. Therefore, I still consider China's interests would not be best served by taking such action. That said, on the battlefield, I do not envisage such armaments making one iota of difference. Western tanks, long range missiles and artillery, military tactical training, and ultimately F-16s plus helicopters will be the ultimate game changers during Ukraine's Spring counter-offensive.'

'I can but hope you are right Witoria. Radek are you regularly returning from Mielec home to see Alexandra and your young family?'

'No General. My visits have to be impromptu – a morning here and there or maybe an afternoon for a few hours. The sheer volume of armament deliveries throughout the day and night means I am forced to be available twenty four seven, especially with rapidly changing munitions requests from Ukraine's Military. As things stand, my first weekend since January in Niepolomice is most likely to be over Easter.'

'Many thanks for your contributions. I now have much cause for thought as I fly back to Warsaw - time for us all to leave Lady and Gentlemen.'

Once on the plane, with Radek left to address and firefight the latest random deliveries coordinating what items are for temporary inventory or immediate shipment, Lieutenant-General Politczek turned to Jan Chmura. 'If I was 'the Surgeon', my assassination contract would be closed over the Easter weekend. You need to consider additional protection measures for Radek.' Jan nodded.

'I assume Witoria you have picked up no further chatter from Kadyrov and his associates or even on the dark net or through other external intelligence sources as to who this man or woman is, what he or she looks like, his or her whereabouts, or even if the Chechen contract has been accepted?' 'General we have no further information since locating that dark net advert for an assassin. We have even put resources into monitoring Kadyrov's frequent visits to Abu Dhabi but again have found nothing.'

Chapter 23

The Surgeon had over the weeks of walking daily past the Król compound covered much of the forested area to its rear. He had methodically checked out each section looking for anything that would assist him in fulfilling his contract. A kilometre and a half from the Król properties he had found an abandoned wooden shed. Pulling open one of the double doors, the Surgeon was pleased to find it was empty rather than filled with broken furniture or obsolete machinery. Pacing out the length and width, it was clear the building could safely house an estate car or sports utility vehicle. Some four hundred metres from the shed on flat, but dry ground, there was a track leading away from this part of the forest. The Professor followed the track, which was neither rutted nor wet under foot for a kilometre as it wound its way gently on a downhill gradient to a single track tarmacadam road. Checking on his map, a broad smile crossed his face. This would ultimately be his escape route after killing Radek Król.

Peter van de Berg began searching websites for an estate car with four wheel drive that was three or more years old. The vehicle had to popular in the Polish Market and should not attract any attention from a passing pedestrian or the Police. Hence, a Porsche Cayenne for example was not on his shopping list. He was also searching for a particular private seller of such a vehicle. He had no wish to be caught on camera in a car showroom. He wanted a private owner who would swallow the story that he wanted to drive the vehicle back to his Swedish home close to the Lund University campus for his daughter over the Easter Holiday. With a pile of twenty thousand euro notes or more or even less in front of such an owner, would that owner agree to let this seemingly harmless Swedish Professor of Architectural History drive the vehicle back to Sweden on their Polish insurance and paperwork? Peter also wanted to take physical possession of the vehicle on Maundy Thursday, the day before Good Friday.

Searching internet sites for four wheel drive estates like the Skoda Octavia was unlikely to help as Peter needed to find such a vehicle locally not in Gdansk or elsewhere. Many Poles advertise their cars are for sale by simply placing an A4 sheet of paper on a rear passenger door window. Such a 'For Sale' signs contain all the usual details that any prospective buyer would need namely mileage, availability of service history, expiry date of the necessary Government road test approval, and of course price.

As Professor Lars Andersson, Peter was a familiar face and common sight in centre of Niepolomice often with his well-groomed golden retrievers. He was after two months absorbed as part of the local scene to the extent when a local asked 'Who is that?' the response was now consistently 'Oh a Swedish Professor investigating our Hunting Lodge's history.' Strolling through the car park, there were always a few cars self-advertised for sale by their owners and it was simply a matter of time for a vehicle close to his criteria, or close enough, was presented. It was a time for patience and a cool calculating head.

Peter needed to establish from Tauron, the national Polish electricity supplier, how the Król Compound receives its power. His rented house provided the excuse to call out the Tauron engineers. Built immediately after the 2nd World War, the wiring in the building was long overdue for replacement. Indeed it was in some ways an accident waiting to happen in terms of being a fire risk if not a danger to the life of any occupant. It was no surprise that the recommendation was for the entire building to be rewired with modern breaker boxes and importantly a new power line from the nearest or most appropriate sub-station.

Armed with Tauron's paperwork, the Professor visited WOZNIAK, the Letting Agents. It became clear that the owner, an elderly Lady, did not have the financial resources to have such work carried out or subsequent redecoration. However, this situation fitted into the Surgeon's future assassination plans in terms of the demise of his alias as Professor Lars Andersson. More importantly in discussion with Tauron's engineers, he had established precisely where the power supply points were in the immediate area and to the Król compound.

Having found the abandoned shed, the Surgeon checked daily for any signs of human activity in and around the building. After it became clear, this section of the forest was neither frequented by other dog walkers nor anyone else, the Surgeon fitted a strong padlock to a newly bolted fitment across the double doors. He took great care to avoid any fingerprints being on these items and the doors using not only again nitrile gloves but also wiping the items and doors with a chemical agent before and after fitting. Easing the Volvo forward, the Surgeon then pulled away from the shed to the track.

Chapter 24

Poland's Prime Minister was looking for answers as to how Russia's GDP growth forecast for 2023 and 2024 by the International Monetary Fund was possible. Forecast or not, the implication was Russia's GDP would keep pace or better the very Nations that had supported sanctions and thus impacted their GDP expectations. If that was not bad enough, those countries refusing to impose sanctions, or ignore them or find ways to work round them, were expected to outperform the forty nine Nations, including Poland, attempting to impede Putin's War of Choice. Sanctions were seemingly not having the impact the West had sought. Economic warfare against Russia, including sanctions, disinvestment, asset seizures, oil price caps, and other measures designed to cripple Putin's economy and war machine, would, according to experts, still need time to take effect and then become increasingly cumulative in their severity across all of Russia.

'Colonel Hanko, I understand from General Politczek, that within ABW's strategic intelligence community, I might personally obtain clarity on why Western Sanctions are yet to impact seriously the Russian economy?'

'Prime Minister, sanctions have certainly caused damage along with the exit of many multinational corporations. In addition, trade bans have already disabled Russia's automotive and technology manufacturing industries. Nevertheless, the Western sanctions announced at the outset of the war were billed as draconian and, inspite of further additions over the last 12 months, your reasonable question is whether they are working or not?

Russia lies about its numbers so disruption may be far worse than admitted. Secondly, Russians have unsurprisingly found loopholes and devised work-arounds so as to avoid sanctions. This has been with the help of Western enablers and other Nations. Thirdly, the initial energy sanctions were counter-productive because they resulted in price spikes delivering windfall profits for Russia. Finally, Russia is not a country but a criminal organization. It is no different to the Mafia and run by oligarchs with Putin as *the capo di tutti capi (the boss of all bosses)*. A Government hiding from Global Law enforcement as it steals from the State's coffers whilst these ill-gotten gains are converted and laundered into Western currencies, real estate, securities portfolios, and big boys toys like private jets and yachts.

There is no evidence to indicate that Western sanctions have influenced Putin's determination to crush Ukraine. Similarly, the impact of economic sanctions has not been so severe as to unleash domestic unrest in Russia, or even challenges in the Kremlin to Putin himself. Members of the Duma parliament, Kremlin officials, and scores of businessmen, including the wealthiest of oligarchs, have all been subject to travel restrictions and to threats of Western investigations and prosecutions, including mansions and yachts being seized. However, such parties are merely inconvenienced whereas actual confiscations of assets would actually hurt the owners. Forfeiture actions by prosecutors have been few. Providing strong evidence to the Courts that the property is associated with criminal activity and the proceeds of crime is for now a stumbling block. As democracies upholding the Rule of Law, we cannot it seems simply change the law to suit this purpose and for the monetary value of such confiscated Russian assets to be devoted to help the reconstruction of Ukraine. Yet it is meaningless unless large-scale confiscations can be made. So far, the scale of such forfeitures runs in the millions of dollars not the billions that could make a real difference. Should we really be making the presumption in law that any Russian ownership has been acquired from criminal activity and putting the onus on such ownership to prove otherwise? Apart from opening a minefield of litigation, at what point subjectively do the monies become laundered clean if ever?

History has shown economic sanctions against numerous countries over many years have failed to ensure greater international security from Iran to North Korea. More recent sanctions on individuals appear to have failed to reverse the massive flow of illicit finance from countries run by authoritarian regimes into the West's major capital markets. To date, the two most effective prohibitions have been the freezing of Russia's foreign exchange assets in Western central banks as well as the removal of Russian banks from the Swift transfer system. Whilst this has damaged Russia's financial system, the rouble, credit ratings, and market values, the only way for the West's sanction policy to win is to attack Russia's energy revenues. This is now beginning to work since the placing in December of price caps on its oil and in February caps on its diesel fuel exports. Oil and gas account for more than half of the

Kremlin's revenue, 50 percent of Russia's export earnings, and roughly 20 percent of the country's GDP annually. Russia is spending roughly US$300 million a day on its special military operation while for most of 2022 it earned US$800 million a day from energy exports. Caps have brought inflated prices down dramatically and Europe has nearly weaned itself from Russian natural gas imports. Gas sales will be down to zero and will remain there helped by fuel and source switching. The introduction of the oil cap on December 5th has already caused Russia's revenue to crash to $200 million a day from $600 million daily. Oil caps on Russian oil have been an ingenuous way to keep petroleum flowing into global markets whilst avoiding another price spike. Roughly seven million barrels a day continue to be exported but this production is now being sold at a discounted price to the cap. China India and others of course benefitting.

U.S. Treasury Secretary Janet Yellen said at the G20 meeting in February that … *we've continued to see emerging markets negotiate deep discounts on Russian oil which keeps oil in the global market, but sharply reduces the Kremlin's take. The way I see it, our sanctions have had a significant negative effect on Russia so far. While by some measures, the Russian economy has held up but Russia is now running a significant budget deficit. The caps we have just set will now serve a critical role in our global coalition's work to degrade Russia's ability to prosecute its illegal war. Combined with our historic sanctions, we are forcing Putin to choose between funding his brutal war or propping up his struggling economy.*

The impact of multinationals wholesale exit on Russia's economy should not be ignored. These companies had in-country revenues equivalent to 35 percent of Russia's GDP and employed 12 percent of the country's workforce. Unfortunately, the 49 countries that have imposed sanctions account for only 60 percent of the world economy. The rest are trading with Russia. Even so, Russia's deficits are growing quickly and its war industrial base is unable to resupply its armed forces with ammunition, spare parts, and weaponry. Provided China remains on the side-lines militarily in terms of supplying armaments and Russia goes broke, the Kremlin will be forced to stop its war. Unfortunately, such predictions at this point in time amount to wishful thinking but make us realise more than ever that Ukraine must win on the battlefield.'

'Thank you Colonel. General Politczek do you have any thoughts on the military situation in Bakhmut before my meeting with the Minister of Defence and our High Command?'

'Bakhmut delivers in my opinion a stark message. The two sides are fighting different battles. Russia plods along into graveyards of its own making where it shows no regard for human lives, including its own. Meanwhile, Ukraine is ferociously defending its territory at great human cost while also increasingly utilizing all of the tools of modern warfare - from advanced technology to superior intelligence. Russia is stuck in the 20th century while Ukraine embraces 21st century flexible combined arms combat. Since Russia's offensive in the Donbas began in April 2022, its army has moved from outside Severodonetsk to Bakhmut, a total of seventy kilometres. That is less than the distance from

Krakow to Katowice. Russia's capture of Bakhmut in eastern Ukraine, if and when that happens, will be the grim culmination of over an eleven-month campaign to take the town with no strategic value at a cost of thousands of soldiers killed and injured. From Russia's perspective, Bakhmut has taken on symbolic value in terms of the Kremlin's propaganda machine touting a so-called victory. Yet, the reality is the campaign has not demonstrated any improvement in Russia's military performance. Continuing to pour in a lot of ill-trained and ill-equipped troops into the Bakhmut battle while Ukraine has been patiently building combat power is nothing to celebrate if you are Russian. The Ukrainian High Command has recognised Russia's way of waging war remains rigid and unchanging. Russian strategy is to utilize massive barrages of artillery, rockets, missiles and air attack in attempts to pulverize Ukrainian defensive positions. This historic tactic was of course used in taking the burnt out, levelled, and uninhabitable cities of Mariupol, Severodonetsk and Lysychansk last year. Nevertheless, Ukrainian military commanders have decided to hold their defensive position in Bakhmut and to further reinforce those positions. Russian forces are facing up to 70 per cent casualties or more in its daily attacks yet Russia's General Staff take no account of their losses in trying to take Bakhmut by ground assault. The Ukrainian Army defending the city has moved, from considering a tactical withdrawal to new defensive positions established during the last eleven months, to inflict as many losses on the Russia's Military as possible. Every metre of Ukrainian land is costing hundreds of Russian lives.

Bakhmut is becoming an emblematic repeat of Stalingrad for the Ukrainians rather than the Russians.

Wagner, the private mercenary group led by Yegveny Prigozhin, have been a bit more effective than the Russian Army, neither though have performed well nor been exemplary in combat. Russia cannot seem to learn from its experiences that it can only move forward when taking unsustainable losses. The addition of the Wagner fighters has complicated Putin's war of choice. Prigozhin and Wagner are proving to be a thorn in the Kremlin's side, apart from further demoralizing Russia's regular army. There has been little to no coordination with the Russian High Command and Wagner. Yet Wagner is taking a larger number of casualties and even suffering, we understand, numerous friendly fire incidents in the small space of the battlefield. This only adds to the atrocious morale within the new conscripts and regular troops leading inevitably to poor battlefield decisions and performance. Russia's overly rigid command structure and the openly mutual hostility between the Army's High Command and Yegveny Prigozhin will not lead to battlefield coordination with shortages of everything due to disrupted and unreliable supply lines.'

'Thank you General – you make Bakhmut sound more like Thermopylae from the Ukrainian perspective whereby Russia's Political and Military Will to fight, when accompanied by the much vaunted Spring Offensive by the Ukrainians, will finally evaporate along with Prigozhin.'

'I very much hope so Prime Minister.'

Chapter 25

Lars Andersson was enjoying a coffee at an outside table in front of a Niepolomice Cake and Coffee shop. The dogs were at his feet also enjoying the warming sunshine after their morning walk in the forest behind the Król compound. He was reading *Dagens Nyheter, Sweden's newspaper of record*, when his eye was caught by Kazakh journalist Azamat Maytanov's syndicated piece. *The chief kidney specialist of the United Arab Emirates, Dr. Yassin Ibrahim El-Shahat, a well-known and highly regarded doctor with 30 years of experience of treating patients with such ailments, has arrived in Grozny. His area of expertise lies in the care of kidneys from dialysis, transplantation, glomerulonephritis (damage to the tiny filters inside kidneys – the glomeruli), and acute renal failure. Ramzan Kadyrov has allegedly been suffering from serious and severe kidney problems that are rumoured to be terminal.* The Kazakh journalist cited his own sources for the reporting.

From the Surgeon's perspective whether Kadyrov lived or died was irrelevant. It was a matter of payment for completion of the contract. This edited piece, which may or may not be true, did though trouble him. Nevertheless, this was not the time for encrypted phone calls, emails, or texts as the piece could well have planted by ABW, Poland's

Intelligence Service. Was it an attempt to draw him out from his elaborate deep cover, establish where he was, and how close the assassination might be? In financial terms, a net three million dollars plus would still be far better than breakeven should the balance not be forthcoming for whatever reason. It was time to keep his nerve and to tie up some loose ends.

Whilst his inclination was to kill Astrid Johansson and thus also her unborn child, Peter still needed her to report any further inquiries from Poland about Professor Lars Andersson up until shortly before the Easter Weekend. It was time for Hans Fischer to once again visit her in Lund and complete the planning of her disappearance, albeit with Astrid alive!

Astrid was fortuitously Danish and she wanted to return to Denmark. Her friends and family came from Aalborg Region more than four hundred kilometres from Copenhagen. She wanted understandably to return there for such local support. In the knowledge of what Fischer had told her at the start of her covert recruitment, affording a home of her own and also being financially independent was very much the promised reward for confirming Professor Lars Andersson as a Faculty of Architecture member. Utilising the Data Protection Law, Astrid had received her Personnel File in the University's Human Resources Department offices. This included her original job application together with details of her education including her degree from Heidelberg University in Architectural History. She substituted documents with totally false and misleading information removing any employment references in the process. In addition, Astrid was allowed as part of Sweden's

145

Privacy Law to access the computerised records enabling her to delete any lead to where Astrid Johansson came from, apart from Denmark. Astrid was a tall blue eyed pretty blonde in her mid-twenties who was very much a loner. There was no one in whom she had confided or could know anything about her or her family connections in Aalborg. Her resignation letter stated that, whilst still in her mid-twenties, she wished to see a world beyond Scandinavia.

Similarly, Astrid had handed in her notice meaning her last day in the Rector's Secretariat would be immediately before Good Friday. She had found a new-build house on a land plot recently completed for sale in Nørholm Enge, a rural suburb of Aalborg. Astrid was delighted not only as access to Limfjord *(a body of water cutting through Jutland)* was less than a kilometre distant from the house but also particularly when her Aalborg Family's Lawyer confirmed completion had taken place.

Returning to Niepolomice, the Surgeon reflected. The property, including all transaction costs, was under US$ 200,000 and when also including a US$100,000 bonus, this had cost him less than sub-contracting the task of having her killed, a win-win for them both.

Chapter 26

As part of Radek's oversight role in assisting the Polish Logistics Corps Senior Officers in its huge task of receiving day and night armaments from NATO members and others, it was essential to see for himself how the Ukrainian Army was performing on re-supplying its front line. A call to Colonel Stepan Nalyvaichenko had them both 36 hours later in Vuhledar. For Stepan, any excuse to escape his subterranean office under the Government building in Kyiv and then be close to the action made Radek a most welcome military companion. Vuledar was once a prosperous mining town and home to fifteen thousand people. Today it was a wasteland with blackened apartment blocks towering over deserted and pock marked streets flanked by partially demolished properties. A church had been reduced to a hollowed out shell with its roof peeled off and windows shattered. Its cross still stood at the front but punctured by shrapnel while in a nearby long deserted playground, there were bullet holes in the slide. Radek, who had fought in Afghanistan and seen the human suffering in north east Syria, saw what was now completely obvious to any observer that Russia hates with a vengeance Ukraine's cities, towns, villages, and even hamlets let alone its people. Such Russian actions only confirmed, as far as Radek was concerned what Stepan of course already knew, the military and political strategy was simply to wipe Ukraine and its people off the global map; ethnic cleansing by any other name but with the added crime of senseless and wanton destruction.

Radek was once more in his full combat gear without any badging indicating only that he was in fact anything other than a regular soldier. Officers were a specific target for Russian snipers. Stepan pointed out that Vuledar had had a natural advantage over the Russian enemy because it was on high ground. The Ukrainian Army had been targeting rail lines used by the Russians for resupply with heavy artillery while holding the bastion that is Vuledar. The front line was one kilometre away from their observation post as the outgoing rattle of heavy machine-gun fire continued. The lack of available heavy armour on the battlefield was apparent. Radek needed to expedite both the training of tank crews and delivery of those Leopards, Challengers, and Abrams heavy tanks. That said, whilst not quite Spring, the ground was already mud-like making life difficult for heavy armour of either side to be fully effective. With undoubted pride, Stepan pointed out where a previous Russian attempt to take the town in the preceding month had ended in heavy losses and humiliation. A column of tanks and armoured vehicles in plain sight had headed straight for Ukrainian defensive positions through minefields. The Russians had been stopped in their tracks somewhat similarly to how the enemy's armoured column approaching Kyiv last year was repelled. Prior to leaving Vuledar, Stepan handed Radek from the back of the jeep a Hecklar & Koch 416 assault rifle together with a 9mm Glock 19 pistol. Radek filled the pouches covering his body armour with ammunition clips for the HK and shells for the pistol. Going to Bakhmut was where the fighting was now at its fiercest along a 1200 kilometre front line. Radek was unsure whether the body armour and weapons were solely for protection or if Stepan's often voiced wish to kill invading Orcs (the Russian invaders) was an opportunity not to be missed?

Stepan and Radek followed carefully a Ukrainian Army Sergeant leading a squad of eleven soldiers to within 500 metres of the front line. The Russians had no line of sight as they were shielded by partially destroyed buildings as two mortars were quickly assemble to lob munitions at designated Russia positions. As quickly as this action took place, the squad moved equally as fast before becoming a target for the enemy. Suddenly there was a warning shout to take cover as sound of a Russian drone was amazingly heard above the constant sounds of shelling and detonations. Tightening the chin strap of his helmet with explosions of incoming artillery and mortars as bullets zinged through the air, this was no longer facing the Russians from the relative safety of a Vuledar observation post. The merciless destruction of residential and other buildings was before their eyes. Bakhmut was yet another broken Ukrainian town without water, heat, or light. Frozen in time and a place with only the elderly remaining - senior citizens' were clinging to memories of times past in order to survive. Old people frightened by shelling and now condemned to a twilight existence living in cellars; humanity waiting patiently for twice weekly food aid deliveries and now facing death simply because they have nowhere else to go. Stepan must have second guessed what Radek was thinking as he shouted above the noises of war '... this town was quiet, calm, and clean. People worked and had money. What more can we say?'

Bakhmut's and Vuledar's demolition into rubble from Russia's constant artillery shelling has been replicated across many parts of the eastern front. The Russians are clearly not winning Radek thought but they are not giving up either. One year after the invasion, Russia still holds almost a fifth of Ukraine that is still, even with that illegal occupation, a vast country on its own account. This is the cold hard truth. Yet in Bakhmut's case, for many long months, this small industrial city in eastern Ukraine had been pounded by Russian Artillery. There was not a single building as far as he could see that did not wear the hallmarks of war. Why Radek asked himself are Russia and Ukraine fighting so hard over what is now a pile of rubble? Why are both sides laying down the lives of so many of soldiers to attack and defend Bakhmut in a battle that has lasted longer than any other in this war? If Military analysts are correct that Bakhmut has little strategic value why on earth is so much blood being spilt and treasure wasted? It is not a garrison town or a transport hub or a major centre of population. Bakhmut held seemingly no particular geographic importance in his mind as an incoming shell blew apart an already semi-destroyed building opposite from where Stepan and Radek were now crouched. This brought Radek back to reality that he was in a live combat zone amongst the debris and dust of urban warfare. The Sergeant leading the squad had mounted his rifle pointing directly ahead. This was the infantry hand signal meaning the enemy was in sight. His next hand movement was an open fist showing his thumb and two raised fingers indicating 300 metres followed by the dispersal signal to take cover.

Stepan gestured for Radek and the five infantrymen behind them to crouch and follow him to the other side of the street. Entering through a doorway with its door long since blown to oblivion, the troops moved quickly through the partially destroyed floors ensuring no infiltration by enemy forces. Stepan then placed on the first floor with a shell holes rather windows and open sky above two soldiers, one with a heavy calibre machine gun and the other with a sniper rifle where both infantrymen had an arc of fire across the comparatively open ground of a former square in Eastern Bakhmut. Downstairs, Radek had positioned the others in similar shielded positions and ordered them to fix bayonets. Interestingly, none of these Ukrainian soldiers questioned Radek's authority to command. Stepan joined Radek on the other side of partially demolished wall cradling his Fort 224 sub-machine gun. Radek had ensured each man had replacement ammunition clips at the ready together with grenades. His orders were clear to each man – 'Fire at will but kill with every shot'. Stepan had given a similar order to the soldiers on the 1st floor acknowledging that the heavy machine gunner had to decimate the on-coming enemy. This fight was about kill or be killed.

Stepan had, to be fair, not expected or intended to expose Radek in this way to such clear and present danger. In mitigation, entering an active and hot urban war zone will always by its very nature be dictated by contact with enemy. The squad had been heading to relieve a forward unit and the plan had been for them both to return with the rotating unit. What had clearly happened was that a probing incursion by the enemy had slipped between forward positions leaving no choice for their squad but to hold, destroy, and then wait to be relieved. An impromptu trap had thus been set by the quick-thinking of the squad's Sergeant. As they waited to engage the enemy, it became apparent to Radek as to why the Russian Army and the

151

Wagner mercenaries had had to deploy major military resources into its continuing attempts to take the City with only limited success. Urban defenders had the tactical advantage of being able to hide in thousands of locations and pick buildings, windows, alley ways, and even sewers within which they remain undiscovered until such defenders choose to engage. Western officials had estimated, as he already knew, that between twenty and thirty thousand Russian troops had been killed or injured so far in and around Bakhmut alone. Within the next hour, Radek would witness at close quarters why the Ukrainian Army in this defensive setting had a kill ratio of at least 7 to 1.

The Ukrainian snipers, using compressors, in both buildings began to fire more than a single round at increasing speed from their over-watch positions. Stepan whispered to Radek '... Wagner scum'. Yevgeny Prigozhin had staked his reputation and that of his private army on seizing Bakhmut. His expectation had been that his fighters, who had been deployed at the Kremlin's behest in Syria, Libya, the Central African Republic (CAR), and Mali on the side of forces aligned with the Russian government, would perform far better than the much vaunted regular, but conscripted, Russian Army. Wagner tactics had been to throw human wave after human wave of fighters at Ukrainian defences resulting in a huge loss of life resulting the decimation and hollowing out of Prigozhin's Private Army's effectiveness. This resulted with the Kremlin's permission for Prigozhin to recruit thousands of convicts from penal colonies in last quarters of 2022. If such criminals joined Wagner and survived for 6 months, the Russian State granted them a full pardon for whatever their crimes may have been. However, Wagner soldiers, whether or not criminals from earlier war crimes or simply people released from Russia's penal colonies to Prigozhin's Private Army, can only go forward. Retreat is not possible as Wagner will shoot anyone attempting to retreat. Hence the more rapid fire of the snipers could only mean a Wagner assault was underway as the Russian Army was now far more circumspect and addicted to attritional shelling whereby everything habitable was converted to rubble. It made no sense for Radek or indeed anyone as to why you would invade anywhere having turned the land into uninhabitable debris.

Short bursts of heavy machine gun fire joined that of the snipers as Stepan, Radek, and the other infantrymen took aim and fired. The Wagner advance continued with the occasional bomb crater or pile of rubble in the Square providing for very few of them only temporary life-saving cover. Nevertheless, waves of Wagner people kept pouring into the square only to be cut down by what had become a fusillade of accurate fire. Radek was reminded of early evening duck shooting with Tomek, his father. The squadrons of ducks would keep circling in the dusk light before diving headlong into the pond. There, in the hide, Tomek taught his son to kill only what they could eat or pass to friends. Here human beings were being slaughtered like rats in a barrel at the behest of political masters as he pulled the trigger again and again on his Hecklar & Koch ending another Orc's life. The sound of bullets embedding in the walls and ricocheting around them made Stepan aware that in a matter of minutes hand to hand fighting would take place. Shouting above the noise of battle, Stepan told them all to look to disable then kill – relatively unprotected arms, shoulders, legs, and feet before saving a bullet and cutting their throats. This was the brutality of war as the Ukrainians to a man yelled *'Slava Ukrayini' – Glory to Ukraine*. Radek followed Stepan through the shell hole before becoming lost in frenzy for survival. As suddenly as the encounter had started it was just as quickly over. Yet the acrid smell of blood, explosions, fear – excrement and urine, and death hung in the air. The fog of war did not alter the facts. Across the square the slumped bodies of Wagner mercenaries lay dead – there were no wounded. Prigozhin was not, Radek believed, going to succeed with such high casualties. Whatever political benefits he was hoping to achieve either directly with Putin or the men of influence in the Kremlin as a potential successor to Putin were becoming less and less achievable. Prigozhin's criticisms of Russia's Defence Minister's, Sergei Shoigu, tactics together with equally public complaints about the lack of recognition for Wagner's contribution on the battlefield and the inadequacy of ammunition supplies had hardly endeared him to the Kremlin Loyalists that included Shoigu. This was now a political struggle for influence being played out in the urban struggle that was Bakhmut and its surrounding villages. The Ukrainian losses were 3 dead, 1 badly wounded, and 4 with minor injuries. As they waited to be relieved, a military medical team arrived to deal with the casualties and take away the dead. Placing inert bodies into body-bags and then strechering them to a parked army ambulance some 300 metres away including the severely wounded soldier was a difficult task. Honouring the living and the dead while negotiating streets covered in varying quantities of debris and rubble was part of the fight.

Radek watched as the ambulance disappeared from view as Russian artillery shells continued sporadically to fall near their position. His throat was parched as if he had crossed a desert. Taking a long pull on his water bottle, Radek's adrenalin was slowly returning to normal and his heart was no longer thumping. Stepan handed him a lighted cigarette. The Kremlin needed, it seemed, a symbolic victory, as, since the Russian forces seized cities like Severodonetsk and Lysychansk in the summer, subsequent territorial gains had been incremental and extremely slow. In addition, the successful Ukrainian autumn counter offensives around Kharkiv and Kherson had forced Kremlin propagandists to look for any battlefield success - howsoever small or irrelevant in the scheme of things. Smoking that welcome cigarette, Radek asked himself, slowly looking at the dead human beings across the square and strangely still, was such a political goal worth the sacrifice of these men and the thousands of lives of others already lost? From a Russian military perspective, there was 'hope' rather than reality that the fall of Bakhmut would provide a springboard to threaten the larger urban areas of Kramatorsk and Sloviansk. In speaking with Stepan, the main strategic purpose is to use the battle for Bakhmut to weaken Russia's army by killing lots of Russians. According to him, as long as retaining Bakhmut allows the Ukrainian Army to destroy more Russians proportionately than they can inflict on the defenders, there would be no tactical withdrawal. Without doubt, Ukraine has sucked and tied up Russian forces that otherwise could be deployed elsewhere along the front line. In addition, the fierce defence of Bakhmut has bought the Ukrainian High Command time to strengthen its defensive lines to the West of the City. This would prevent any breakthrough by the Russian Army if such a tactical withdrawal from Bakhmut became strategically necessary. Furthermore, the assembly of major battlegroups with heavy armour, long range artillery, and mobile infantry vehicles has continued unhindered for the well-telegraphed Ukrainian counter offensive this Spring. Stepan had reminded Radek that Ukrainians also would be withdrawing into additionally strengthened defensive zones in the Kramatorsk Region, ten years in the making. In addition, Kramatorsk itself is situated on higher and more defensible ground than Bakhmut making any advance likely to be every bit as bloody for the Russians as its campaign for Bakhmut. Certainly, Western officials' estimates of Russian troops, including Wagner mercenaries, killed or injured so far in and around Bakhmut were entirely possible in Radek's mind given his recent encounter with Prigozhin's Private Army.

Radek spent the next four days with Stepan visiting numerous stockholding armament centres in the Donbass learning what problems were being encountered with shipments from Mielec's inventories. Ammunition deliveries seemed to be the greatest concern from rifle bullets to artillery shells. Consistency of deliveries was stressed by everyone as increasingly important. The planned counter offensives were already placing additional pressures for stockpiles to be built up substantially. Deliveries to the battlefront from critical logistics hubs, like Chasiv Yar, do face incoming Russian howitzer shells intermittently. Yet Radek witnessed such long-range fire had not deterred or stopped Ukraine's Armed Forces carrying ammunition, food, fuel and reinforcements to the front lines. The roads between Chasiv Yar, Slovyansk and Kostiantynivka were all passable for Stepan in his military four-wheel drive Toyota Land Cruiser with military traffic in both directions. The rotational Ukrainian combat units he encountered in the Chasiv Yar sector appeared to be well fed, in good spirits, and well disciplined. Radek and Stepan were frequently offered hot drinks by these rotational troops whilst pointing out to them nearby building basements as bomb shelters. Most if not all soldiers appeared to be rested, clean and well-armed with a mix of NATO-standard and Soviet-era equipment. Morale was high. Formations were holding against continuing Russian infantry attacks in and around Bakhmut with Russian assaults lacking heavy weapons. Radek heard time again of a willingness to stand and fight the Russians every step as long as Polish Logistics can keep delivering Western ammunition. He also heard from soldiers relating frontline experiences that Russian troops were taking crippling casualties. Entire platoons and even companies effectively were being wiped out in daylight assaults against fortified positions backed by drone-controlled Ukrainian artillery and mortars. Units holding defensive positions long-term did suffer bit-by-bit losses but, for the most part, replacement troops once the formation rotated from the front line were then back-filled.

Heading back to Poland from Kyiv by train, Radek noticed a Reuters report stating that the Russian Duma had enacted a law pushing back the age bracket for compulsory military service from the current 18-27 years to 21-30. This would mean during the transition period between the old legislation and the new for the years 2024 and 2025 would see the conscription age span 10 or 11 years rather than the usual nine. Meaning only more young Russians would be eligible to fight and be killed senselessly he thought for no good reason.

Turning the page of his newspaper, Poland's Commissioner for Security of the Information Space was reported as having accused Russia of utilizing false pacifism to advance the Kremlin's interests. The Polish Agency responsible for information security claimed Russia was applying this tactic to influence the global audience for a temporary pause in its war on Ukraine; a pause only to enable the Russian Army to rebuild and regroup before recommencing hostilities. Russian media has ramped up its covert financial support for European pacifist movements that propose there should laughably be a cessation of hostilities for humanitarian reasons. These elements of false pacifism were consolidating around pro-Russian groups in Poland and elsewhere promoting narratives in line with the Russian propaganda efforts. Such tactics are another component of Russia's psychological pressure to persuade the West to decrease its support for Ukraine. Radek found himself bristling with anger that his country could have allowed Russia to foster such self-serving peaceniks who were motivated solely by receipt of roubles or more probably dollars. After the sacrifices Ukrainian civilians and soldiers had already paid for freedom and democracy, Poland should, in his view, name and shame these people publicly as liars and traitors – they were not fit to call themselves Poles. His mood did not lighten as he read Major Oleh Yurchenko's obituary – a Hero of Ukraine who had recently been killed in Bakhmut. A man who had heeded the call to arms in defence of his country and his death was still a heavy loss no matter how many Russians are killed. Radek read and reread his 22 year old daughter's, Olesia Yurchenko, words spoken at his funeral *'... it is about everyone cherishing the virtues of hard work, kindness, honesty, loyalty to one's country, and their family – that is what my father taught me. Not to give up, not to retreat and remember we still have to build the country ... build Ukraine'*.

Chapter 27

A Polish Military Hercules landed at Warsaw's Frederic Chopin Airport from Rzeszow. Radek had jumped an early morning ride on the transport so he could report directly to Lieutenant-General Politczek on his recent visit to Ukraine's battlefront. President Duda's recent announcement that four Soviet-made MiG-29 fighter jets in full working order were being immediately handed over to Ukraine with the remaining MiGs being prepared for shipment after being fully serviced, had been met with pleasure by Poles and Ukrainians alike. Importantly Poland's President had made the point that Ukraine's pilots would be ready to use these planes in combat instantly. When Slovakia's Prime Minister, Eduard Heger, announced that its 13 MiG-29s would be shipped in the next few weeks, the general mood in the intelligence services of the Bucharest 9 improved. Western Capitals had been slow to recognise Russia's Imperialist ambitions unlike the '9'. Ukraine is defending the front line of the free world and failure to support its defence will mean the front line will move ever closer. Kyiv still needs more assistance to win the conflict. People in Ukraine are dying so for the Bucharest 9 intelligence services there was no longer any room for politicking by any Western Government if Ukraine is to remain a viable state and survive as an independent democratic nation. Hopefully Radek thought the politicians

would remember the Slovakian Prime Minister's words that
'... *both Governments stand on the right side of history*'.

Congregated once again in the General's 8th floor
Rakowiecka Street office, Radek commenced proceedings
with his overview of the real situation on the battlefront and
the logistic wrinkles that the Polish Army's Logistic Corps
were already addressing in Mielec and Rzeszow.

Jan Chmura began his summation of what had been
an important week for ABW's counter intelligence service.

'Our Interior Minister, Mariusz Kaminski, announced
earlier the charging of six foreign citizens with preparing acts
of sabotage and spying for Russia. These foreigners were
Belarussian, Russian, and indeed Ukrainian who sought to
disrupt military and aid supplies to Ukraine. In addition,
proceedings are being prepared against ten other people
detained in the operation. Evidence acquired during
searches of premises occupied by these people indicated
that this spy network was monitoring railway lines with
sabotage very much in mind either in Poland or even
Ukraine. The cell's tasks included recognising, monitoring,
and documenting weapons' transports to Ukraine and then
preparing sabotage actions aimed at severely disrupting if
not paralysing the supply of equipment, weapons and other
military aid to Ukraine. These six suspects have already been
charged with conducting espionage for Russia and
participation in an organised criminal group as part of our
ABW operation. Our officers found cameras, electronic
equipment, and GPS transmitters that were to be mounted
on aid transports to Ukraine. The latter would of course have
exposed such trains and the lines themselves to Russia's long

range missile attacks once on Ukranian soil. What was particularly pleasing was finding direct evidence proving that the Cell's paymasters were Russian Intelligence. Our people did also find some cameras near Rzeszow airport that we believe were part of this Cell's commencing surveillance activity. We found similar connecting evidence at both our Mielec Airbase and the new railheads. With military and cargo aircraft from the United States and across Europe regularly fly in and out of Rzeszow and Mielec, we have increased security perimeters and in conjunction with our Army's military police, seen more patrols day and night. These sites and immediate areas have thus become highly sensitive since the February 24th 2022 invasion and on-going ground security issues. With regard to the latter, thorough sweeps are now taking place on every military shipment, whether by freight train or truck, prior to departure as Radek can confirm, together with heightened military police security within the entire area. '

'Jan, memory tells me that Patriot air defence systems to protect theses sensitive areas are already deployed?'

'Correct General – nevertheless our decades-long spy conflict between Russia and us has only intensified since the Ukraine War began back in 2014. We have arrested close to twenty people on suspicion of spying for Russia since the 2nd invasion. A few months ago another Russian citizen, a man who was registered as a long-term resident here, had spied for Russia between 2015 and 2022. Our investigation found he had collected information on the organisational structure of our military units in the north-east of the country. Similarly, a Spanish national of Russian origin, who was later identified as an agent for Russia's military intelligence agency (GRU), was arrested in Przemysl, by us late last year on suspicion of spying for Moscow. Whilst the success of the recent operation is welcome, Russia, after targeting its military forces on Ukraine in 2014, it also unleashed its intelligence services on the United States from interfering with its 2016 elections to cyber-attacks to poisonings and sabotage in Europe. I am very worried, as are my Baltic colleagues, about who the FSB and GRU spies have already activated let alone their agents still embedded as *sleeper* agents. We are recruiting across all levels within ABW. However, rooting out these traitors already embedded in Poland is a never ending challenge in peacetime for any democracy but in war it is now a necessity.'

'Jan is right General. Yet as this covert war has intensified, Western countries have sought to hit back inflicting lasting damage on Russian intelligence's effectiveness. The unprecedented expulsion of five hundred Russian officials from Western capitals symbolises that impact. These individuals may be described as diplomats when the reality was the majority were Russian undercover intelligence officers. People tasked with cultivating contacts and recruiting agents who can pass on secrets – traditional espionage. Today, Russians are employing what are described as *active measures* ranging from spreading propaganda to more aggressive covert activity. We expelled of course forty five Russians for just such activity focussed on undermining Poland's stability. As Jan has indicated, man-marking an individual spy is resource intensive and expensive work. Although as we know, Western spies in Russia have long been subject to round-the-clock surveillance whilst their Russian counterparts in Western capitals have not. The recent expulsions are more than a symbolic gesture of protest but part of the wider push to degrade Russia's capacity to do harm. Such mass expulsions are long overdue as the larger presence, the more difficult it is for all Western Intelligence agencies to keep track on what the Russians are up to and planning. A number of our European neighbours have taken serious steps by expelling so-called diplomats to reduce the Russian intelligence services capability and threat. Since 2014, Western intelligence agencies have been successfully coordinating and working to identify Russian spies resulting in Germany for example expelling closer to one hundred Russian intelligence officers. In addition, such cooperation has ensured anyone expelled cannot simply apply for a visa in another Western country. The volume of expulsions over a relatively short period has had a debilitating impact on Russian intelligence services that has led to embedded agents being activated. That said, the invasion of Ukraine may provide solid opportunities to recruit from within the Russian Intelligence agencies as disillusionment grows about Putin's War of Choice. Nevertheless, since 2014, Ukraine has been the epicentre for more brutal covert struggles with not only each side trying to recruit and root-out spies but also with assassinations of high-ranking Ukrainian officials. These spy battles could still escalate further such as, we have seen, targeting supply lines bringing in military aid for Ukraine. I believe a missile strike on convoys or facilities in Polish territory is low risk but sabotage could be attempted in Poland given our key role as a staging post for military hardware going into Ukraine. Such clandestine operations are often carried out by Russians who travel in and out of a country so our Border Force has to be on high alert. Similarly, the remaining intelligence agents still in Warsaw's Russian Embassy provide the enabling infrastructure so our surveillance definitely needs to be intensified.

Western Nations, the European Union, and the G7 partners should intensify their attacks on Russia's lucrative fossil fuel export revenues and throttle Putin's ability to fund its ongoing war in Ukraine. A lower cap on Russian crude oil exports is needed to apply more pressure on the Kremlin. Sanctions on the top powerful banks in Russia are yet to be sanctioned by the West, for example, Gazprombank. We could do a lot more as a collective West to put further pressure on Russian finances. The joint European Union-G7 measure set a maximum purchase price of $60 per barrel for seaborne Russian crude oil this December that coincided with an EU and United Kingdom ban on seaborne Russian crude oil imports. This was swiftly followed by subsequent EU-G7 price caps on other refined petroleum products in the last month. Whilst a good development that the oil prices cap has been set, $60 per barrel is actually still too high. Russia has simply no technology to limit or stop oil production from its drilling facilities. Restricting or even halting oil production at wells in some of Russia's maturing fields creates problems when idled for a lengthy period of time. For example, Russia's benchmark Urals crude blend is made up of oil from multiple fields meaning its quality might be altered and price reduced if some Russian wells are closed. Clearly, a large-scale reduction in oil production would do severe damage to Russia's upstream production capacity. It would render tens of thousands of marginal wells uneconomic and compromise complex pressure management systems at the field level. A risk recognised by Russian reservoir engineers but less evident to Western Governments, apart from the knock on effort of deeply undermining political support for the Kremlin in Russia's oil producing regions. Ukraine has of course been pushing for a cut in the oil price cap, along with our Baltic friends and us. We have to go further and we have to squeeze this price cap to the lowest possible level. It should be noted that Russia kept selling during the COVID-19 slump at a price $16.6 per barrel for Urals crude. Recent economic indicators suggest the Russian economy, which at times has appeared more sanctions-resilient than we hoped for, is struggling to maintain its lucrative fuel exports in a falling export market. Russia's budget deficit is also widening amid higher military spending and falling fossil fuel revenues reaching over $34 billion as of early March and its Finance Ministry reporting oil and gas revenues 46.4 percent lower than 12 months ago. Our Government has to be more assertive General.'

'Well I will raise these facts about the oil cap in particular during my Monday Meeting with the Prime Minister. However I would be interested to know from any of you what you make of the International Criminal Court (ICC) issuing this morning an arrest warrant for Russian President Vladimir Putin on charges of war crimes?'

'My understanding is Hague investigators worked on evidence against Putin for over a year before the ICC issued this arrest warrant. It accused the Russian President of being allegedly responsible for the war crime of unlawful deportation of Ukrainian children and their unlawful transfer from occupied areas of Ukraine to the Russian Federation. Though any chance of Putin actually standing trial in the Hague is extremely unlikely, General.'

'Whilst Radek is I believe correct, the arrest warrant does though send an important message to many Russians whether in the military or pro-Kremlin media pundits about the possibility of facing war crime charges. There is, I am told, a lingering sense of dread amongst Russian propagandists about the growing likelihood of facing arrest warrants and ultimately War Crimes Tribunals. The Kremlin's propagandists have plenty of reasons to be concerned by the manner in which they have been willing participants in state-controlled media in prompting, encouraging, rationalizing, and even normalizing Russian acts of aggression and genocide against its next-door neighbour. Extreme talk, for example, spouted by Russian-state controlled media led to Anton Krasovsky's sacking from Russia Today (RT). During an October interview, Krasovsky spoke of drowning Ukrainian children while setting homes on fire before he turned to talk of rape. This caused outrage in both Ukraine and Russia with the RT's Editor denouncing such statements as *wild and dangerous*. Even so, other Russian talking heads have not only justified violence against Ukraine but have also suggested the use of nuclear weapons against the United States and other Western nations over their support for Ukraine. Since the ICC arrest warrant has been issued for Putin, there is undoubtedly a serious panic now across Russian Media as to what comes next. There is no going back to the way things used to be. There will be more arrest warrants issued, not only against Putin but others In the Kremlin and Media. The reality will be that such people could be arrested whenever they get off of an international flight or if and when Putin's Regime collapses.'

'I think Witoria is right General. When we consider ICC Investigators have been assembling evidence since the atrocities first came to light by the Russian Army in Bucha alone to subsequent indiscriminate use of internationally banned cluster and other munitions to specific targeting of residential properties to destruction of hospitals and schools, pro-Kremlin media supporters have every reason to be equally concerned and nervous as personnel in the Russian military undoubtedly are. The ICC has shown a persistence and perseverance to bring such criminals to trial even if many years pass.'

'I speculate that many of the countries in the General Assembly plus a number of the nations that abstained in the recent United Nations vote have acknowledged the sovereignty of the ICC. For a man like Putin, who sees himself bestriding the global stage on Russia's behalf, his ego will be impacted by an inability to travel to many countries without risking immediate arrest as an accused war criminal. Putin will definitely not be travelling to any of the 123 countries already signatories to the ICC's jurisdiction. Arrest, incarceration, and ultimately extradition to The Hague to stand trial wait for him. These ICC countries include 18 Eastern European, 25 Western European, 33 African, 19 Asia-Pacific, and 28 in Latin America and the Caribbean apart from a few more within the 141 in the United Nations General Assembly denouncing Russia's invasion. Certainly, Belarus, North Korea, Eritrea, Mali, Nicaragua and Syria are hardly on my bucket list as places to visit whether on business or pleasure. Many thanks again for your insight and briefing'. Lieutenant-General Politczek closed the meeting to some chuckles and laughter.

Chapter 28

Gazeta Wyborcza lead stories were President Xi's State Visit to Russia described by China's Foreign Ministry as a *'Journey for Peace'* and President Putin's weekend visit to Mariupol. The Surgeon was once more in role as the Swedish Professor as he sipped an espresso between turning the newspaper's pages. He had watched the previous evening a television clip on Polish Television showing Putin driving himself into a residential area of Mariupol, meeting residents, and viewing what appeared to be a new apartment within that residential complex. Something did not feel right. Why was there no security detail accompanying the President of Russia with other road access not blocked off? With 90% plus of Mariupol destroyed at the end of May last year, was this newly built residential development even in Mariupol? Was the person on the television clip shown beforehand on Russia's Channel 1 a doppelganger rather than Putin himself? President or double, there were very few if any words uttered from his lips during his visit. Similarly, when meeting a few of the so-called residents, there words were addressed to him but not responded to by nods of the head. The Surgeon decided the entire visit had been stage managed with a double and actors for propaganda purposes to indicate to the Global Community that Russia's President was continuing his duties unaffected by the ICC arrest warrant. As for the new residential complex, was it credible that such a large development could have been built in eight months? The Surgeon thought the most likely answer was a stage set with digital cutting and editing, especially as the alleged visit to Mariupol was conducted during the hours of darkness. As for the reported daytime visits to Rostov on Don and Sevastopol were other doubles used? With President Xi's State Visit about to commence, was it realistic that over the weekend before Xi's arrival, Russia's President would embark on a panoply of visits? The Surgeon decided for himself that the weekend visits were entirely fake news solely for consumption by the comatose Russian people of another dose of Kremlin propaganda than anything to do with the ICC Arrest Warrant.

Like many towns not only in Poland, there are people, who have dropped out of society whether from losing a job, divorce, mental instability, drug or alcohol misuse, bad luck, poor choices, or whatever and thus become homeless. The Surgeon had noticed in the small park in front of the Niepolomice Castle that in the early afternoon a group of two to four alcoholics would gather on one of the park benches. The faces might change but the group always remained in an alcohol induced stupor. Drinking cheap vodka as the afternoons wore on, talking shouting and singing amongst themselves until the inevitable argument caused a disturbance requiring Police intervention. Most townsfolk gave these homeless people a wide berth either moving in the opposite direction or hastily entering a shop. Sometimes people could simply not avoid the drunk shuffling towards them asking for money. The Surgeon had identified one of these homeless people, who would irregularly appear, disappear, and then reappear weeks later, as being not that much different in size and height to himself physically. The man, who was Polish, answering rather bizarrely to 'Marco' as opposed to a more commonplace christian name like say Mateusz or Pawel in Poland, was riddled with fleas and lice. His unkempt appearance was made worse by his overgrown beard and unruly mop of shoulder length hair before even breathing in the unhygienic sour smell of body odour. An unsettling smell created from many months of sleeping rough outdoors in the same multi-layers of clothing through the winter.

Whilst finding a 'Marco' or someone like him was an integral part of the Surgeon's assassination planning, gaining such a man's trust let alone cleaning him up posed serious challenges for the Surgeon. In addition, seemingly befriending this 'down and out' should be done in such a way that he attracted no untoward attention from locals or the authorities. His covert status as that *amiable Swedish Professor with two retrievers* could not be risked.

Handing any 'down & out' a 20 zloty banknote would merely make the donor an immediate target when next sighted in Niepolomice. Begging was just as much an essential part of such homeless people's survival as finding a night shelter. As the Surgeon considered the few safer options but all with a degree of risk, a visit to Krakow, that included visiting a charity shop where a pair of second hand jeans, shirt, and fleece together with new socks and boxers, bought him some time mull things over; how to mitigate such threats to completing Kadyrov's contract caused by the need for a 'Marco'? The Surgeon decided that handing 'Marco' money, of whatever zloty note denomination, would merely end up as vodka down his throat or even worse injected in an arm. Therefore, providing takeaway food like zapiekanka, pierogi, bigos, or even soup or pizza occasionally was a better option in building that trusting relationship. Convincing a man like 'Marco' to take a shower after years of living life in shop doorways and elsewhere was still a major hurdle. It was no surprise the local swimming pool and sports centre refused any homeless person access to their shower facilities – calling immediately for security if not the police to repel any attempt to enter. 'Marco' was of course riddled with fleas and lice with an unkempt, if not repulsive beard and an unruly mop of shoulder length hair.

Whether the weather was warm or cold, the Surgeon determined that 'Marco' would have to be thoroughly cleansed in the garden of his rented property. All his clothing would need to immediately burnt as he was being hosed down whilst utilising dog shampoos for lice and fleas, body wash, and soap. In Kaufland, the Surgeon bought towels. In addition, whilst in that store, he bought electric hair clippers and scissors to deal with the man's beard and hair. A decorator's set of overalls for his personal protection, rather like a hazmat suit for dealing with dangerous substances than a human being, from Castorama completed his purchases.

As the week's progressed, the Professor would slowly provide the drunk known as 'Marco' with food whenever the man appeared. At first, his visits were infrequent and haphazard. As time went by, 'Marco' was seen daily in the park. Interestingly, he would be sitting apart from the other homeless people on a separate bench. The Surgeon noticed that the man was gradually no longer comatose from alcohol but increasingly wanting more food. This led to him feeding

'Marco' with a mid-morning takeaway and repeating the process in the early evening as Easter approached. The few locals, who fleetingly began to take any notice of the Swedish Professor's apparent philanthropy towards 'Marco', considered such human kindness would change nothing and ultimately his good intentions would be abused by this hopeless addict. In fact, the Surgeon was seen more as the victim rather than the Good Samaritan by such locals rather than the grooming of a human being by the Professor for a somewhat different purpose.

The Tauron Engineers had, when checking the electric supply and wiring in his rented house, highlighted how the overall voltage supply was delivered to a transformer substation for subsequent distribution to homes and businesses across the immediate Niepolomice Township. Electricity Pylons are used to support electrical cables transmitting high-voltage electricity from a nearby power station where it is generated. The Surgeon followed the path of these steel towers across the undulating landscape for four or five kilometres. Parking his Volvo in a passing point along a narrow country lane, he let out the retrievers for a walk towards small woodland that was crossed by a number of towers. Once out of sight in the wood, the Surgeon identified two towers that if blown up would ensure the lights would definitely go out across Niepolomice. These fifty metre tall steel structures were at their base secured into concrete foundations. The surgeon had already created improvised electronic devices whereby the semtex explosive could be detonated using a mobile phone. Hence this visit was to ascertain in daylight where the explosives should best be placed to ensure each tower would be completely toppled after detonation. The dogs provided yet again a plausible alibi for his surveillance activity and also the ability to warn him of any human presence nearby by their boisterous barking. Placing a test charge on one Tower pillar, the Surgeon tested whether the digital detonator would activate and set off a small amount of semtex on receiving his mobile's call. The result was positive – the waiting was almost over.

Chapter 29

Colonel Witoria Hanko was irritated by what she saw as more delay and prevarication by Western Powers in their support for Ukraine's Fight. It was not for once about speeding up armament deliveries or equipment or even provision of the latest fighter aircraft or fulfilling other promises of support. The G7 group of advanced economies had delayed a long-awaited review of its price cap on exported Russian seaborne crude oil. A price cap was introduced in line with a European Union embargo and currently is set at $60 per barrel. Ukraine and Poland together with the Baltic and Scandinavian States, as the more Russo-sceptic states in the Western Alliance, wanted the cap now to be much lower. The Kremlin's lucrative oil income was of course helping to fund, if not fully finance, its attritional and destructive war in Ukraine. Moving the cap to $30 per barrel would, in her view and others in Global Intelligence Services, save lives as Russia's ability to continue funding its war through this oil revenue would be substantially reduced.

Building and maintaining the consensus between the camp of the Baltic States, Poland, and Scandinavian countries and those from the Mediterranean transporting the Russian crude and crude oil products was the United States priority. Whilst American negotiators appeared open to renegotiating the price cap if European Union nations abandoned periodic price cap reviews, the United States changed course much to Colonel Hanko's frustration. There were genuine worries a lower price cap might destabilize the global market, especially when current research forecasted a major increase in demand over the summer. The southern mediterranean European Nations had a general concern that if the price cap goes lower, the transportation business will then swiftly move into the black market. Advocates of revising the cap downwards say that Russia will still sell its oil even at reduced prices. The Kremlin had as a matter of fact previously continued to send its crude to market when prices were much lower than they are today. Whilst the $60 per barrel price cap has eaten into Russian profits without upending the market, Colonel Hanko and others still believed now was the time to be turning the screw. The G7 countries measure prohibits anyone providing services, from financial to transportation to insurance, for Russian crude oil and oil products if sold above the price cap. That figure was to be reviewed every two months with the European Union already prescribing the cap should be at least 5 percent lower than average market rates. When the weighted average export price of Russian crude was $52.48 per barrel, excluding shipping and insurance costs, the Americans stance could be understood even by the Advocates wanting a lower cap. Yet United States Treasury Secretary Janet Yellen had stated the price cap coalition was committed to re-evaluating the agreed price point in March. Colonel Hanko knew her Ukrainian friends in Zelensky's Government wanted the review to happen. However, the Ukrainian Government felt time should be allowed to achieve a consensus decision for a significant downward movement in terms of the price cap.

Kyiv wanted the new cap set at $30 even though other countries believed it should be at the level of around $50 per barrel. Hence, continuing discussions to achieve a far lower price made sense. The United States was not, as Colonel Hanko knew, against cutting the price cap but wanted to shore up consensus for any new price point.

Colonel Hanko updated her briefing note on the Oil Price Cap for Russian crude and crude oil products for Lieutenant-General Politczek, and ultimately for the Prime Minister, and pressed send on her laptop. She turned her attention to the demand of more than thirty states, including Poland, for the establishment of a special tribunal for the crime of aggression. Aggression is one of the core crimes under the jurisdiction of the International Criminal Court based in The Hague. The Court's legal definition is *'the planning, preparation, initiation or execution, by a person in a position effectively to exercise control over or to direct the political or military action of a State, of an act of aggression which, by its character, gravity and scale, constitutes a manifest violation of the Charter of the United Nations'.* Colonel Hanko noted by this definition this crime is ascribed to individuals rather than nations. On this basis, Putin and other senior political and military officials could probably be indicted and then prosecuted.

As she considered the probability of such charges being made, the Human Rights Commission of the United Nations had forwarded the findings of an Independent International Commission of Inquiry on Ukraine. It documented in painful detail wilful killings, unlawful confinement, torture, rape, and unlawful transfers of detainees from the illegally occupied areas that came under

176

the control of Russian authorities in Ukraine. The report highlighted a widespread pattern of torture and inhuman treatment committed by the Russian Military against the people they detained including cases of sexual and gender-based violence involving women, men, and girls, aged from 4 to 82. The report also specified rapes were committed at gunpoint, with extreme brutality, and with acts of torture such as beatings and strangling. Perpetrators at times threatened to kill the victim or her family if any semblance of resistance was shown. Colonel Hanko recognised these barbaric actions were neither incidental nor accidental. Indiscriminate shelling of civilians, wilful killing, and torture together with sexual violence, looting and forced displacement on a massive scale were designed to spark fear and terror into the civilian population. Ukraine's Prosecutor General's and the ICC Prosecutor's teams had collated details on over sixty five thousand war crimes from the evidence of atrocities committed in Bucha, Irpin, Mariupol, Izium, Kherson, Kharkiv and other liberated cities and towns together with mass burial sites in areas occupied by Russian troops. Colonel Hanko felt disillusioned by the sheer scale of the task of bringing all those responsible to face justice in spite of the determination of the Prosecutors.

Nevertheless, the earlier issue of arrest warrants for President Putin and his Commissioner for Children's Rights (Maria Alekseyevna Lvova-Belova) by the International Criminal Court lightened her mood. The warrants were issued for the war crimes of - the unlawful deportation of population (children) and the unlawful transfer of population (children) from occupied areas of Ukraine to the Russian Federation. The kidnapping of over fourteen thousand Ukrainian children is a war crime that cannot go unanswered. Such actions harked back to the days of Stalin where deportations were part of the Russification of occupied territory. An insidious policy of ethnic cleansing linked to cultural genocide - clearly a central pillar of Putin's and the Kremlin's Imperialist Strategy today.

Witoria Hanko was feeling sick and depressed before turning her attention to the fact Russia was about to assume the chair of the Security Council. The United Nations had provided, without the shadow of any doubt, a platform for Russian propaganda over the past year. She recalled the monotonous rebuttals of fact by Vasily Nebenzya, the Kremlin's Ambassador to the United Nations. Chairing the Security Council gives Russia yet again the opportunity to set agendas and make appointments that will at the very least consume needed time and deliberately divert public discussion away its obvious and continuing crimes against Ukraine. Interestingly, as the Ukrainians have pointed out over recent months, a case can be made that Russia has no right to chair the Security Council at all as the Russian Federation has never formally joined the United Nations. Furthermore, whilst the Soviet Union was a permanent member of the Security Council, the Soviet Union is not today's Russia and the USSR ceased to exist more than thirty years ago. Why does the Russian Federation assume it has such automatic status she fumed? All of the other post-Soviet states were either already members of the United Nations as former Soviet republics (Ukraine or Belarus) or went through the application procedure to join. Russia had never in fact applied; perhaps relying on bully boy tactics of the country had the largest nuclear arsenal? Ukrainian diplomats refer to Russia as *occupying the seat of the former Soviet Union* – precise but correct she thought. Russia's formal role at the United Nations had provided cover for its malign activities but Witoria could not foresee in the short term the General Assembly unanimously voting to remove Russia's permanent membership of the Security Council. In her mind, and probably correctly, the Russian State would have to embrace democracy and the Rule of Law thereby ending endemic corruption under communism that had simply continued on Putin's watch by him and his acolytes – the senior siloviki and oligarchs. Would there ever be a Russian Media focussed on the facts, reality, and truth in her lifetime as opposed to a constant barrage of State fed propaganda? What chance did an ordinary civilian Russian, educated or not, have of accepting and realising Russia's Government and Military High Command were war criminals?

Colonel Hanko cut a forlorn figure as she left ABW's Rakowiecka Street Headquarters in the late afternoon. The Finns were right she thought with their saying '... *that nothing good comes from the East only Sun'*. She needed some shots of vodka and something to eat in the noisy environment of a nearby bar to clear her mind momentarily of the Kremlin's disruptive and harmful impact on the world let alone its own people.

Chapter 30

Walking through the parked cars in Niepolomice's town centre, Professor Lars Andersson found what he had spent many weeks searching for. A Volvo Estate not dissimilar to the one that had first brought him to Niepolomice back in late January with a 'For Sale' sign sellotaped to a kerbside rear passenger window. The details indicated the car had been bought from new and serviced at Krakow's main dealership. A recent full service at 180,000 kilometres and Government Roadworthy test told him all he needed to know. He phoned the contact number.

The vehicle's owner had recently retired and was looking to better the price a dealer would pay. His asking price was twenty six thousand euros. The Professor and owner agreed to meet and for a test drive to be undertaken. Afterwards the offer of cash and with no negotiation on the price was unsurprisingly doubly attractive to the Volvo's owner. The Professor's reasons for wanting to conclude the transaction on Thursday prior to Good Friday were entirely plausible from the owner's perspective. In the run up to the Easter Festival and holiday, the Professor did not wish to be a hostage to any difficulties in international banking transactions regarding his funds being remitted. In addition, as he had voiced during their discussions, his intention was to drive the Volvo back to Sweden over the holiday. Arrangements were thus agreed to conclude the transaction on Thursday Morning.

During Thursday afternoon, the Surgeon drove to the woodland that he had reconnoitred previously. He took a collapsible lightweight ladder from the boot and proceeded into the small copse of forest. The retrievers were willing assistants in terms of forewarning him of any unwelcome human presence as he began the task. The Surgeon fitted the semtex charges and digital detonators to each leg of the electricity supply pylons. He tested again the burner phone and its link to the other charges before wrapping a weather proof covering around them with duck tape. This was a painstaking process requiring the wiring to be suitably protected into the actual charge from the variables of Polish weather at this time of year. By the time, the last charge was secured and checked, it was already dusk even with the benefits of the clocks recently being moved forward one hour.

The following morning the Professor walked with the dogs into the centre of Niepolomice. It was Good Friday. He handed over the cash and took possession of the Volvo. As requested, the owner had filled up the tank. With the retrievers in the boot space, the Surgeon proceeded to head directly for the abandoned hut that had become his temporary base. Reversing carefully, the Volvo was now garaged with the keys left in the ignition.

Walking back across the parkland to his rented house with the dogs, the Surgeon noticed additional protection people within the Król compound. There were usually two on display with another two either in one property or split. Now there were four visible indicating a move to a day and night rotation requires at least 8 officers he thought. Otherwise little had changed in the target zone. As he was apply the leads to the dogs' collars, a large military Mercedes saloon passed by – his target had arrived.

It was by now midday as the Surgeon entered the garden to be met by 'Marco'. The retrievers for once made no rush to greet a human being for a boisterous welcome. Whether they sensed the man was riddled with fleas and lice or his smell might also put them off, they settled under an apple tree some eight metres away. The Surgeon had promised 'Marco', if he came at lunchtime, not only would he be fed but also, subject being cleaned up, a hundred euro note. Money for a man who was homeless it seemed a small fortune.

The Surgeon handed 'Marco' a sandwich while he lit a fire. His instructions were simple - strip and throw all your clothes into the fire, everything including boots! Once naked the Surgeon played a hose connected to the kitchen mixer taps constantly over 'Marco'. The water was thus warm as the man began shampooing his hair and beard before using body wash. The products were identified as being effective in removing fleas and lice permanently. After ten minutes, the Surgeon rinsed off the remaining soap suds and threw 'Marco' some towels before making him sit on a garden chair. Taking a pair of sharp scissors, he cut and threw into the fire large clumps of his hair and beard. After this the electric clippers tidied up both his hair and beard before 'Marco' was subjected to more hosing, shampooing, and body washing for another ten minutes. Fresh towels were handed to him to dry off before being handed the clean clothes to change into with new boots and socks. As the last set of towels joined the others on the fire, the Surgeon doused the embers and clothing with more petrol. Quite how 'Marco' felt as he went into the house holding that 100 euro note, one will never know as the 'Surgeon' injected him with a lethal dose of sodium thiopental in the neck as they crossed the threshold. Setting an unconscious 'Marco' upright in a worn and old winged armchair as his life was drawing to a close; the Surgeon then called in the dogs to receive their lethal doses. A distinctly macabre scene of corpses was thus staged in what was the parlour off the kitchen – Marco now dead with the two retrievers seemingly asleep at his feet.

As darkness fell, the Surgeon began to set the stage for the entire house to be engulfed by fire in the early hours of the Saturday morning. He had to ensure that the fire would completely destroy the house including all the contents and leave only skeletons. Yet in doing so the forensic assessment as to the cause had to lead to the property's electrical wiring being long overdue for replacement. The garage was an integral part of the building with a doorway into the kitchen and parlour. This gave him the opportunity to place three full 25 litre plastic jerry cans of petrol next to a stack of kindling and logs stored in the garage. The Surgeon pushed ripped up shirts as rags into the opened cans leaving the lids on top to melt in the ensuing planned conflagration. Using a large stone, he began hitting the Volvo's petrol tank until an almost imperceptible leak began to appear gradually on the floor. He locked the steel garage doors from the inside using the existing metal beam slotted into 'U' shaped holders before turning his attention to the main and ancient fuse board in the parlour where the electrical energy supplier's engineers had pointed out the possibility of a serious house fire breaking out. The wiring left the fuse board in poor quality trunking that had long since deteriorated in many places. If the wiring started to arc through excessive loading, a fire would spread rapidly across the entire building. The initial flames would follow the decayed trunking embedded in tinder dry lath and plaster internal walls and ceilings. However the Surgeon had to have a reliable trigger to set the entire property ablaze. The gas supply to the kitchen stove entered the building through the basement via an old cast iron pipe. Raising a 3 kilogram lump hammer, he hit the pipe with some force. His hearing picked up a soft hissing sound of escaping gas from no doubt a hairline fracture of the pipe. An instant later bending his nose closer to the hissing noise he smelt gas. He had opened every internal door so that the interior of the building would act as a large flue. Returning to the sitting room, the Surgeon filled the fireplace with an array of logs, adjusted the chimney damper to slow the burn, and lit the fire.

It was shortly before midnight as the Professor left his temporary home of the last 3 months for the last time. Whilst it would have been quicker to have crossed the parkland alongside the Król compound, the risk of being stopped in the dead of night, especially with the additional protective team enabling 24 hour cover, was too high. Hence the Surgeon had anticipated such a situation and had bought a second hand bicycle for this special and final journey. He had spent some time in the previous weeks cycling towards the forest checking out the quickest and safest route to the wooden hut. He had done this not only casually in daytime but also at night. Like many villages and small towns in rural

Poland, by 11:00 pm the only lights visible were street lights especially as this year's early Spring weather still felt like the depths of winter. Safe inside the wooden shed, he painstakingly wiped down the bike to remove any tell-tale fingerprints before placing it ready to be loaded in the enlarged boot space with the Volvo's rear seating down. The Surgeon stripped down to his thermals before layering green temperate camouflage inner and outer wear. The mixture of colours of green, beige, brown and dark grey would hide a slow moving body shape in the darkness of the forest. Similarly, he applied face paint to camouflage his eyes, nose, temple, and chin so as to break up the shape of his face before applying dark brown to his neck and ears. Turning off the campinggaz light, the Surgeon left the wooden hut.

Slipping silently to his pre-chosen observation point, the Surgeon looked through his night vision binoculars across the Król compound towards his rented property. Some forty minutes had passed since he left the house. Yet there were no signs as yet that his work as an arsonist had been effective. Had he miscalculated? As Peter scanned the compound, he saw the two protection officers chatting presumably on a coffee and cigarette break but still nothing on the skyline. Doubts began to surface in his mind and whether 3 months of careful planning was about to prove worthless. He could not return to house for many reasons but walking into a ticking bomb was up there amongst them. This was about exercising patience as he leant his back against a tree with his legs outstretched on the ground to wait.

Back in the house, the gas had filled the basement and made its way slowly into the kitchen and parlour being

185

heavier than air before flowing upwards to the bedrooms on the first floor. The natural airflow within the property had delayed the gas finding its way into the sitting room and integral garage.

The sound of the explosion jolted Peter awake as a plume of flames lit the night sky. He watched the Protection Team's response. They were clearly talking into ear pieces and telling each property's occupants to head immediately for the safe rooms. Shortly afterwards, the two other members of the Protection Team joined their four colleagues in the compound fanning out covering both the front and rear. The officers were not distracted by the sound of fire engines racing to the scene or the subsequent explosions as the Volvo's fuel tank and jerry cans caught alight. The Surgeon had correctly surmised that he was dealing with professionals. The occupants of both houses had been trained not to turn on lights and look out of windows but to head straight for the safe room, using probably Ledlenser night searcher torches, as he saw briefly the flicker of a beam or two. As the Surgeon prepared to leave for the wooden shed, his eyes caught sight of the St Bernards, who were either in a sitting position or flat on the ground, whose heads were ironically focussed on the blaze. The distraction had seemingly only impacted the canine kingdom. Keeping his movements to a minimum, the Surgeon slipped slowly back into the depth of the dark forest and eventually the sanctuary of the wooden shed.

Chapter 31

As dawn broke across Niepolomice, the smouldering ruin of what had once been a detached house, and temporarily the home of the Surgeon, had the fire brigade tenders gradually disappearing. The fire had been extinguished although precautionary hosing was still taking place in part to cool what was left of the building's structure. The Police Forensic team arrived mid-morning together with the Fire Chief to begin painstakingly analysing how and why the property had seemingly exploded causing damage to nearby residential properties with windows blown in.

The Protection Team were clearly on high alert. However, the absence of any visible threat or attack on the compound or the homes of Radek and his parents during the hours of darkness made the officers begin to lower their guard. By mid-afternoon, the local Police Superintendent had received verbal reports on site from both his Forensic investigators and the Fire Chief's assessment. The General View was the Professor and his dogs had been overcome, whilst probably sleeping, by a slow gas leak. A fracture in the original basement cast iron pipe bringing gas into the building was seen as the most likely cause of the escaping gas. With windows closed because of the return of winter weather, the gas gradually flowed through the building with ignition emanating finally from the embers in the sitting room fireplace. It was felt the Professor and dogs had succumbed from tiredness to be being rendered completely unconscious by the deadly effect of leaking gas. This had prevented their movement from the parlour to the sitting room. PGNiP, the gas supplier, confirmed that the cast iron supplies into the residential properties along the street were scheduled for replacement with high-density polyethylene in the second half of the year. In addition, TAURON, the electricity supplier, had provided its earlier assessment of the wiring and fuse-board being long overdue for replacement. The lack of proper maintenance and repair was in reality the root cause of the Professor losing his life. The Police had contacted WOZNIAK, the Town's 'only Residential Property Agency for sales and lettings regarding the ownership. The story was a common Polish one of an elderly people having died leaving the property to their children or relatives who could never agree on what to do from renovation and ultimate sale to a straight sale as the house stood. Letting, even in the building's poor condition, was the only option agreed upon by these beneficiaries. It would at least cover the property taxes and limited expenditure. The matter was of course made worse as a sibling had died with the result that his interest was inherited by his children. As for the explosions, the Fire Chief considered the spread of the fire into the garage ignited the Volvo's petrol tank causing a further explosion after the initial gas blast together with the jerry cans petrol melting to engulf the stored logs and garage into a fireball. The failed electrical trunking also assisted the spread of the fire to be extremely rapid between the floors as more natural gas flowed into the building. By the time the brigade had arrived on the scene, their task was simply to contain the conflagration and to stop the fire spreading to nearby properties.

The Surgeon would have been more than delighted to have heard both the Fire Chief's and Police's assessment of how and why the fire had occurred. By late afternoon, the Protection Detail was also totally at ease as they explained what had actually taken place to Radek, Alexandra, Tomek and Ewa.

'A false alarm then' said Tomek

'It would appear so' responded the senior Protection Officer.

Chapter 32

Waking from a deep sleep in the back of the Volvo, the Surgeon began to make breakfast inside the wooden hut. It was lunchtime. His first task afterwards was to prepare his CheyTac M200 Intervention sniper rifle. After fitting the suppressor, that would virtually obliterate the sound of firing a shot to a click, he loaded 0.408 cartridges into two box magazines, seven per box. The AMG scope was already on the rifle suitably tested and adjusted from previous test firings during March at ranges of 1400 to 1600 metres. Using disposable nitrile gloves throughout to avoid inadvertently leaving any partial or complete fingerprints, the Surgeon continued his cautious and careful approach. His ghillie camouflage suit hung on the wall to which he began to add random pieces of vegetation. Turning to his backpack, he loaded a couple of water bottles together with an AMG digital spotting scope plus bars of chocolate before tying down a rolled thermal ground sheet. The Surgeon then steadily made sure everything in the garage was stowed in the Volvo. There may well be no time when he returned to do nothing else but jump in the Volvo and leave if he was to live. He removed the padlock and fitting so the shed doors could be easily pulled open revealing his getaway vehicle, the recently acquired Volvo! Finally, it was attending to those comfort break matters as he could be waiting for many hours before the opportunity of a kill shot on Radek Król presented itself.

Carrying the CheyTac 200 weighing 15 kilos whilst wearing a ghillie over his camouflage clothing together with his backpack through the forest and its undergrowth required extreme fitness. His movement was slow and purposeful with periods of stillness before he reached his chosen position some twenty metres from the edge of the forest. Once his thermal ground sheet was in place, the Surgeon adjusted the tripod on the CheyTac and the rear pod in the rifle butt while also checking the bubble lever on the scope for the gun to be absolutely level. With the ghillie covering his entire prone body, the Surgeon was invisible to the naked eye. Nevertheless, remaining still was always a sniper's priority. Any movement could draw the unwanted attention of the Protection Detail or indeed the occupants of the compound properties or an unknown third party. With an overcast sky and a cold north easterly wind, it felt like minus 2 degrees with the wind-chill. Lying flat on the ground in a prone for hours would inevitably mean muscle stiffness from such inactivity if not cramp. Nevertheless, the Surgeon had attempted to counter such problems by layering from thermal underwear to cushioned camouflage winter combat trousers to a cashmere black rollneck sweater under his arctic combat jacket. However, swallowing a prescription skeletal muscle relaxant was probably his most important final act as the hunter waited for his prey to appear.

The Surgeon was amongst many things an observer of human behaviour. Curiosity is one of those key impulses driving humanity to understand what it knows and what it does not. Over the last few hundred years, curiosity has become the desire to know more. Albert Einstein, probably the most intellectually brilliant scientist of the 20th century, stated about himself *'... I have no special talent – I am only passionately curious'*. The Surgeon knew at some point that natural curiosity would become too hard to resist for Radek Król in particular, let alone his wife. It would not matter that his Protection Team and Police had indicated everything there was to know about the explosions and fire at the Professor's house. Furthermore, there would be nothing more to be gained or gleaned from looking at the blackened ruin closed off by police tape first hand. Yet that innate human curiosity would guide them inexorably to the ruin at some point in the afternoon when the heightened anxiety of the previous night would have morphed into relief, calm, and ultimately peace; a natural feeling for both the Króls and also their Protection Team. A mid-sixteenth English Proverb *'Curiosity killed the cat'* aptly described this very human condition – warning in just a few words of the dangers of unnecessary investigation, particularly when there is no need for any such inquiries.

During the early afternoon, he saw brief glimpses of Radek Król. These sightings became more frequent whether taking turns with his father mowing the large expanse of lawn around the properties or cleaning up after the dogs; sadly with giant breeds what goes in one end remerges from the other. The Protection Officers were meanwhile passing occasionally binoculars between one another to make scans of the common parkland and forest boundaries as mugs of probably hot coffee were passed around. The Surgeon was beginning to think his plan to draw out the Króls had been fundamentally flawed as dusk was only an hour away. Swallowing another skeletal muscle relaxant tablet and biting into a chocolate bar, Peter van de Berg was cold and every muscle tendon and brain cell was screaming *'let's go'*. It was then Radek and Alexandra Król emerged hand in hand slowly walking towards the entrance gate – a lover's stroll. Two of the Protection Officers accompanied them to the gate where the other two members of the Team were smoking probably their twentieth cigarette of the day. Passing through the gate held open by those officers, the group made their way to the site of the Professor's former home. After ten minutes or so later, the Króls came back into view with their arms around each other. At around 1200 metres from the Surgeon's position, Radek turned to Alexandra. Taking her in his arms and lifting her up, he kissed her. The Surgeon had his sight on the back of Radek's neck with Alexandra unseen apart from her hands on his broad shoulders. The CheyTac safety was flicked off by a forward movement of his trigger finger as he gently emptied his lungs.

The Protection Officers heard the imperceptible swish of a bullet and turned towards the couple who were seemingly falling to their knees in slow motion yet still in an embrace. It was only the instantaneous sight of blood in that split second which made them react. Dropping to their knees, with pistols in their outstretched hands, they searched for the assassin. Their colleagues arrived sprinting from the gate to discover the Króls were dead from a single bullet. Tomek and Ewa Król had been ambling towards the gate with the grandchildren to meet Radek and Alexandra when their idyllic world crumbled in front of. Dusk was falling as the compound lighting system came on automatically because of the movement by the entrance gate. The Surgeon quietly and methodically left his hiding spot as slow movement gradually brought blood flow into his limbs as adrenalin kicked in. Making his way to the rear of the properties but still within the safety of the forest, the Surgeon picked up a thermobaric grenade launcher that had been hidden days earlier. He proceeded to fire two rounds into each house. The result was four massive explosions with flames shooting many metres into the air. At that moment the compound lights went out with the buried diesel fuel tanks in a matter of minutes also exploded. The Surgeon took out his mobile phone and detonated the charges on Niepolomice's Electricity pylons. The Town was in complete darkness. The Surgeon's heart was pumping fast as he carried the grenade launcher as well. Back in the wooden hut breathing heavily from the physical exertion, he placed the launcher, CheyTac, and ghillie into the Volvo boot. With the gear in neutral he pushed until the vehicle began to move slowly forward. Jumping into the driver's he allowed the Volvo to slowly gather speed without starting the engine. The Surgeon continued to allow momentum to take the Volvo until it reached the tarmac of the lane at which point he started the engine. Taking back roads, he found himself over 2 hours later close to the Slovak border. Pulling off the road, he drove down a small track to an empty parking area next to the shore of Jezioro Czorsztynskie Lake. He proceeded to wade out into the cold water dumping the grenade launcher, CheyTac, and every other item of equipment using the weight of the military equipment to keep all the garments lashed to them underwater. Cold and naked he washed off his camouflage paint taking fresh civilian clothes from his suitcase including ordinary shoes. Back in the Volvo, he checked his appearance. A beanie masked his blond hair and a pair of seemingly thick glasses completed his temporary disguise.

194

Chapter 33

The crouching Protection Team were scanning the entire area as the Compound lights came on. Two officers were easing the lifeless Radek Król off Alexandra Król who was now covered in her husband's blood. Ewa Król cradled Marysia in her arms while holding little Maya's hand as Tomek ran forward to Alexandra, his daughter in law. Holding tightly with his protective arms around here, he looked down at the prone body of his son. Tears were rolling down his cheeks as Alexandra convulsed against him between sobs and uncontrollable screams of despair. No sooner had the compound lights come on than it seemed both Król properties erupted into balls of flame rising many metres into the sky. Everyone either instinctively threw themselves to the ground or was thrown down as the blast wave hit them in the split seconds from the sound of the explosions. As for the Protection Team, the combination of the Compound lighting coming on immediately after Radek was killed followed by the incendiary flames of the burning houses had completely shattered their night vision. When Niepolomice's lighting failed, they were in total darkness except from the light provided by the Króls burning homes.

The surviving members of the Protection Team, one officer had died as a result of flying debris from one of the house explosions while another was severely wounded, moved the living into the Toyota Land Cruisers spiriting them away to a safe house. Two of the officers remained, one with the injured colleague, and the other waiting for the fire brigade, ambulances, and police but not necessarily in that order.

Lieutenant General Politczek was finishing dinner when he was interrupted by Kapitan Stanisław Bak with the news of Colonel Król's assassination. Kapitan Bak knew of the General's fondness for Radek, perhaps as the son he never had, but all within Poland's Military and Senior Government respected Colonel Król the man. Bak had beforehand lit the fire in the General's study, opened a bottle of his favourite speyside whisky (Glenfarclas 25 year old) placing a stuart crystal tumbler alongside on the table next to that worn but comfortable leather armchair beloved by the General.

After giving orders to Colonel Chmura to leave for Niepolomice immediately to be his eyes and ears as to what had transpired, Grzegorz phoned the Prime Minister with the news of the assassination. Shortly afterwards, Kapitan Bak reappeared, picking up the remote to turn on the television. It was the late evening TVN news reporting a major power blackout across the Niepolomice area and two major house fires with reports of two deaths. Pouring another refill, Grzegorz picked up his mobile speed dialling the General Commander of the Polish Police, Filip Zieliński.

'Grzegorz, Inspektor Adek Landa, our most competent, experienced, and successful detective is already on his way to Niepolomice. The President and Prime Minister have already advised me of the Country's sad loss

196

this night and the importance of bringing all those responsible to face justice. You should be aware I have only just come off the phone with Christopher Wray, Head of the FBI, telling me that a Forensic FBI team is already in the air heading for Rzeszow. Grzegorz, I have been inundated with calls over the last hour and a half from our allies with offers of assistance. Radek was much loved and respected by everyone in the intelligence services, the military, and European Governments – we all owe him a duty to hunt down and find this assassin.'

Chapter 34

Adek Landa knew picking up the trail of the assassin would depend on solid detective work and a large modicum of luck. A man in his early fifties, thrice divorced in a catholic society, and a somewhat dishevelled appearance with a lit cigarette seemingly always to hand hardly supported the glowing endorsement by the General Commander of the Polish Police to Lieutenant-General Politczek.

With dawn breaking, Inspektor Landa arrived at the crime scene. The Local Police had cordoned off the entire area and a Forensic Team from Krakow had been working from the early hours in the ruins of the Król compound properties. Standing metres away from where Colonel Król had died, Niepolomice's senior police officer, Staff Sergeant Nowak, confirmed that nobody had been allowed to search the forest for any evidence as to the assassin's presence and identity. A haggard senior Protection Officer was facing up to the reality that, on his watch, his team had failed as a protection detail. Inspektor Landa recognised the introspection and second guessing by the man but he needed his expertise. Walking towards the forest, Adek asked him to accompany him and began to engage him in conversation. The Inspektor soon learnt what had happened the previous evening from the actual shooting to the destruction of the houses to the power cut across all of Niepolomice. As an aside, the Protection Officer mentioned the seeming explosion of a nearby property the previous night. In Landa's world, there were no concurrence of events by purely chance. He did not believe in a world of coincidences after a life spent detecting and solving crimes. The Protection Officer indicated the general area of forest from where both he and his colleagues believed the 'kill' shot had been made. They were standing some eleven hundred metres from the spot where Radek had died. Turning back to the forest, they began to gingerly move through the forest looking for any signs of the shooter's presence. Whilst the assassin would have shot from cover provided by the darkness of the forest, the shooter still had to be sufficiently forward to see through his scope the target. Having used police incident tape to mark the left hand side of the search area, the two men moved purposefully and slowly southwards. After twenty five minutes, they came across flattened undergrowth covered by a thermal blanket.

The Inspektor made an immediate call over his police handset for a Forensic Team to come over to this spot and begin checking for any DNA markers or evidence that might help identify the shooter. The men continued tracking towards the rear of the Król properties, now burnt out ruins. Here they found spent casings of thermo-baric shells and forest undergrowth trampled by someone moving in haste. Another call to the Forensic Team for back-up, they followed the direction of the trail. As the undergrowth gradually disappeared, the forest floor left no trail. The men continued in the general direction, albeit now some twenty to thirty metres apart. It was the welcome shout to the Inspektor from the Protection Officer – the wooden shed had been found.

The Tauron Engineers had found why Niepolomice's energy supply had failed as dusk fell the previous night. Two pylons had been toppled into the woodland that the electrical cables had been crossing. Whilst this was another crime scene, the engineers were under time constraints to re-establish electrical supply to Niepolomice. The Inspektor left immediately with a couple of Forensic Officers to see that crime scene before returning to the site of the Professor's house fire and explosion.

Stood outside the cordoned off area, the Inspektor had been listening to Staff Sergeant Nowak's assessment of what the Fire Brigade considered had taken place. Whilst there had been attempts to contact Lund University, it was Easter and only security personnel were presently on campus. It was then that they were approached by a rather nervous looking man. He explained that the late Professor had bought his white Volvo Estate. He felt somewhat embarrassed to have the cash with the Professor being dead. However, he was surprised not to see his white Volvo still within the curtilage of the property. Landa stopped Staff-Sergeant Nowak attempting to shoo the man away and listened intently to what he had to say. The Inspektor received twenty minutes later a text from the man confirming the Volvo's vehicle identification number (VIN) and the vehicle's registration number. Nowak found the VIN on the burnt out Volvo shell and it was not the white Volvo's.

Taking out a map of southern Poland, Adek considered that, if he was the assassin, he would be looking to leave Poland's territory as quickly as possible. This meant the crossings into Eastern Slovakia. With the further Russian Invasion, both Poland and Slovakia had installed additional cameras not only at the geographic border crossings but also again within one kilometre in either direction. The Inspektor barked his orders.

Chapter 35

President Duda spoke for all the Senior Ministers in Poland's Government and probably all Poles when he said to Grzegorz 'We were unable to honour him properly in Life but we will definitely do so in death'. So it came to pass that on a cold but sunny Monday a week later, Radek was laid to rest alongside his fallen GROM Team 6 comrades from the fight in the Forests of Sumy some 12 months earlier. To say that Colonel Król was accorded full military honours rather understates the pomp and circumstance of the state funeral.

Alexandra flanked by Tomek Król and Lieutenant-General Politczek walked onto the parade ground following the slowly moving gun carriage carrying Radek's coffin and a saddled rider-less black horse with highly polished riding boots set backwards in the stirrups. The symbolism was not lost on any of the individual lines of GROM soldiers who stood at attention with heads bowed as the cortege passed. It signified to everyone a mighty warrior had fallen in battle. As they arrived in front of platform of dignitaries, Alexandra and Tomek walked to their seats in the centre of the first row of mourners while Grzegorz stood in front of the microphone to begin his Eulogy.

'Mr. President, Ambassadors, Alexandra, members of the Król family, and my fellow Poles: There are few events in our life that so unite and so touch the hearts of all of us as the passing of a true hero and warrior. There is nothing that adds shock to our sadness more than his assassination as Colonel Radek Król embodied the ideals of our people, the faith we have in our institutions, and our belief in the fatherhood of God and the brotherhood of man. Such misfortunes have befallen Poland on other occasions in our history but never more shockingly than nine days ago. We are saddened, we are stunned, and we are perplexed that Radek, the friend of all people of good will, a believer in the dignity and equality of all human beings, a fighter for justice, and an apostle of peace has been snatched from our midst by the bullet of an assassin. Yet we do know that this violent act was stimulated by forces of hatred and malevolence. What a price we have paid for this fanaticism. What matters now is that feeling of loss — that personal sense of emptiness — that all of us feel because Radek was cut down in the prime of life. As a country, we have lost a man who understood overwhelming responsibilities of service to one's country and yet discharged his duties with dash and joy, which were an inspiration to all who served with him of whatever rank. Our Nation is bereaved. The whole world is poorer because of his loss. However, we can all be better human beings because Radek has passed our way. His character, his vision, and his quiet courage have enabled him to chart a safe course for us through the shoals of treacherous seas that encompass the world today. Perhaps the indelible mark a man such as Radek Król was his selfless duty and service to Poland and the cause of freedom. There are many people here today from Presidents to Ambassadors to Government Ministers to Counter-

Intelligence Officers to Special Forces officers from far and wide who bear witness to Colonel Król's steadfastness. As I look around, there is no one we would rather have protecting our 'six' than Radek. His bravery was never in question as the many honours confirm but perhaps his greatest contribution to our Country and Europe's safety was his counsel on matters of State. An intelligent man who could have followed a far easier path yet his love of democratic freedom meant serving his Country to the best of his ability. Having survived missions in hostile territories Mali, Afghanistan, and more recently the Forests of Sumy where he was severely wounded, we could not satisfactorily protect our unsung hero on Polish soil. There is anger and frustration in my heart at having to endure such a loss. Yet this is not the time to speak of such things rather how this man touched all our souls. Radek Król was more than that. He was a man filled with the joy of living. He was a devoted husband, a father, a son, a colleague — and finally my friend. If there is a lesson to be learned from this tragic event, if we really love democracy and freedom, if we truly love justice and mercy, if we fervently want to make this Nation better for those who are to follow us, we can at least renounce the hatred that consumes people and the bitterness that begets violence. To Radek's father and mother, to Alexandra and their children, and to the wider Król family - on behalf of a grateful Nation and all mankind, I express our deepest sympathy on this terrible bereavement in the deep expectation and knowledge his selfless example will inspire us all. Colonel Król may you rest in peace alongside your fallen brothers in arms.'

As Grzegorz finished the Eulogy, it was the signal for the parade to be called to attention and to reverse arms with heads bowed in respect for GROM's and Poland's fallen hero. The sound of the 'Last Post' played by a single bugler echoed eerily around the Special Forces Gdansk garrison and line by line of rank and file.

GROM Team 8 were the honour guard alongside the gun carriage carrying Radek's coffin and the saddled rider-less black horse as the muffled drums of the Polish Naval Ceremonial Band began to lead the assembled cortege to the Military Cemetery. It would be there Radek would finally be laid to rest alongside his fallen Team 6 brothers in arms who had lost their lives only 12 months ago in the Forests of Sumy.

Alexandra cut a sad but very beautiful figure, even though wearing black, as she walked behind the gun carriage. She was accompanied by Grzegorz and Major Matt Elliott *(in the dress uniform of a Royal Marines officer)* having been the best man at Alexandra's and Radek's wedding. Behind them came President Duda and President Zelensky with the Ambassadors of the Baltic States, Scandinavia, Germany, Denmark, and France together with the senior members of those countries' intelligence services and military – without forgetting Ukraine's Foreign Secretary and the United States Secretary of State.

With so many foreign dignitaries arriving in Poland, it was hard to keep the press and television cameras away from the ceremony. This forced the hand of the Polish Government to provide some details of Poland's unseen and silent hero. All Special Forces by their very nature avoid being photographed not only for their own protection but also to enable them to carry out any covert mission.

However, with even Polish State television demanding access, agreement was reached State TV would be allowed access subject to ABW having editorial control and the subsequent edited video being syndicated to the other Western TV channels.

For a man who in Life shunned the limelight, Poles had suddenly woken up to the knowledge that Radek symbolised the many Polish sons and daughters who stood on the wall protecting their freedoms and way of life.

Chapter 36

A review of Polish border camera recordings revealed a white Volvo crossing into Slovakia just before midnight on April 8th, Easter Saturday. Closer inspection showed the driver wearing glasses and a baseball cap make facial recognition seemingly impossible. The number plates were unchanged from the Polish registration details which did not surprise Inspektor Landa. Anyone can drive a Polish Registered vehicle provided you have the Registration book with current insurance and road test. Whoever the driver was, this enabled him to drive within the Schengen Area provided he had an identity card and was a precaution if stopped for any reason by the authorities. The Slovakian Police picked up the vehicle with the same registration crossing the border into the Czech Republic. Both Slovakia and the Czech Republic require vignettes to be purchased by any car owner crossing their territories if they are going to use their respective motorways. Whilst these can be purchased on-line, Adek guessed correctly that the assassin would purchase the necessary vignettes as soon as he came across a petrol filling station advertising their sale. Slovak and Czech Police were asked to check the probable garages who had sold the relevant vignette to the owner of a white Volvo estate on April 9th and then to review their video footage with the garage staff. Could a face be put on the assassin?

Forensic reports began to arrive on Staff Sergeant Nowak's temporary desk in Niepolomice's Police Station. Whoever had placed explosive charges on the electricity pylon stanchions had worn gloves which meant no prints were found. As for the explosive used, it was semtex but its composition indicated it was manufactured in the Czech Republic. Traces of urine were found in the area where the assassin had fired the fatal shot killing Colonel Król from which a DNA trace was obtained that matched other imperfect specimens found around the wooden shed. With regard to the destroyed Król properties, the shell casings revealed that the grenades had been manufactured in Bulgaria.

Detective Landa opened again the Fire Brigade and Police Report on the fire that had taken place the night before the assassin had struck. The assessment was that the fire was caused by a gas leak and the occupant, a Swedish Professor and his retrievers had been overcome by the poisonous methane, dying where they slept. It was all too tidy an answer. From Arek's limited knowledge of dogs, their sense of smell would have awoken them and thus their master – it did not add up. Picking up Colonel Chmura's papers on his verifying who Professor Lars Andersson was, contact had been the Rector's Office at Lund University. His confirmatory conversations had been with an Astrid Johansson who seemingly worked in the Rector's Secretariat. The Inspektor picked up the handset and dialled the University asking to speak to Astrid Johansson in the Rector's Office. After a few minutes, a man answered advising him that Ms Johansson no longer worked at the University and left its employment immediately prior to Easter to apparently hitch hike round the world. No one had as far as

Adek knew been able to notify anyone in authority of the Professor's recent demise so he asked to speak directly to the Rector. When he was told by the Rector in no uncertain terms that no one to his knowledge knew or had ever met a Professor Lars Andersson, the Inspektor knew immediately the Professor and the assassin were one and the same person. Thus who was the man found dead in the fire?

The Inspektor systematically began asking the towns people of Niepolomice what they knew about the Professor. Many remembered him as a friendly individual with two boisterous retrievers always happy to pass the time of day. However, it was the Warden of Niepolomice Castle who mentioned how kind he was taking food to the inveterate alcoholic misfits who frequented the seating in the small park outside the Castle. When asked was there anyone in particular the Professor tended to help, the Warden responded that one of this disparate group, who answered to 'Marco', seemed to benefit in particular from the Professor's kindness and largesse. However, he had not seen the man since immediately prior to the Easter Weekend.

Police Staff Sergeant Nowak was considering the weapons and explosives purchased and supplied to the assassin. Whilst there were a limited number of armourers within Central and Eastern Europe servicing the requirements of the criminal underworld, supplying a military grade thermobaric grenade launcher and ammunition would have been a very unusual and specific order. In speaking to underworld contacts, one name kept being suggested as probably the only person capable of fulfilling such a request, Karel Veselý. With the semtex having been manufactured in the Czech Republic, the detectives agreed that this was a good a place as any to follow through on this aspect of the investigation.

Bundespolizei, Germany's Federal Police reported that the white Volvo with the same plates had crossed into France. In addition, photos of the driver filling up with diesel and paying at the till in a petrol station gave the Polish Police for the first time a face for the assassin. However, the trail was about to go cold as the burnt out Volvo was found in some railway sidings in Besancon. Adek Landa was not surprised to learn there were no matches on Interpol's data base and was left wondering if the facial shots were really the assassin's true face or yet another disguise. This killer had been far too careful and meticulous to suddenly be dropping his guard.

It was time with their Czech colleagues to pay Karel Veselý a visit.

Chapter 37

Karel Veselý had read the news reports and seen edited highlights on television of Colonel Król's funeral. Bearing in mind his reputation in the underworld for supplying whatever was requested, Karel knew it was only a matter of time before he was interviewed by the Police. What he did not expect was the suddenness of the Czech Police's entry into his home as dawn broke across Prague. Whether the intention was to make him ill at ease, Karel did not know. Nevertheless, the forced entry into the family home exposing his wife and young children to the full rigour of a police search turning the house upside down did have that result. As Tommaso Genovese had made it abundantly clear weeks' earlier, silence was the only guarantee for his family and him to continue living.

However, the assassination, or rather murder of Colonel Radek Król ten days earlier brought forth an unexpected reaction. In the Police Interview room, he was nonchalant waiting for the arresting Police Officers to either charge him or let him go. His lawyer would be arriving shortly and in the absence of any contraband, drugs, unlicensed weapons, or excessive money, the Police would be forced to release him. It was then four men from the elite Czech 601st Special Forces Group entered the room. Karel Veselý realised instantly the Genovese might kill him but these men would if he did not tell every detail of his encounters with Tommaso Genovese and what he had provided.

Inspektor Landa read the Czech Police Report which also contained a photo fit of Tommaso Genovese's face from Veselý's description. Sadly there were no cameras in the Liberica Café and with the passage of time none of the adjacent street cameras had retained such footage. Whilst Staff-Sergeant Nowak researched just who Tommaso was within the Genovese Mafia clan, the only Tommaso he found was a six year old boy. Both detectives knew they were dealing with a chameleon – a man who was a master of disguise and deception. As they discussed this latest setback in the hunt for 'the Surgeon', Nowak commented how the assassin seemed to immerse himself in each character to the smallest detail. Inspektor Landa grabbed the phone and dialled his Czech counterpart. It was odds on that Tommaso would stay in a luxury hotel as befitted a senior Genovese clan member - perhaps such hotels would retain film for longer periods as a security measure.

Two hours later, the Inspektor received a phone call. Tommaso Genovese had stayed in a suite at the Grandium Hotel Prague and the Czech Police were now working through hotel tapes for that period.

Peter van de Berg had cycled away leaving the burning Volvo to destroy any vestige of anything that my lead the Police to him. He had now adopted the identity of a French National about to enjoy a cycling holiday covering about fifty to sixty kilometres a day. Leaving one hostel for another, Peter would cover the nine hundred kilometres in around eighteen days to the Cote d'Azur and home. The 'velo' cycling holiday routes, as the French called them, were predominantly through countryside and villages away from the hustle and bustle of cities, towns, and autoroutes. A lone cyclist might attract more attention than one accompanied by other people. Every night in a hostel, Peter would befriend whoever was planning to cycle the following day towards his next hostel. As Inspektor Landa entered Lieutenant-General Politczek's 8th floor office, Peter had left the Moselle-Saone cycle route and was following the Rhone southwards. To all intents and purposes for the authorities he had become a ghost - untraceable.

'So Inspektor, what you are saying is that, unless something dramatic happens either from the Czech Police or we have a lucky break, bringing Radek Król's assassin ever to face justice is looking extremely slim?'

'Sadly General, Yes.'

Chapter 38

The news that Radek Król's murder would remain unsolved and become yet another statistic as a Police cold case was hard for everyone to accept. For those who had known Radek, even if only by sight, there was a feeling of emptiness and loss that could never be filled. For his beautiful widow, Aleksandra, one could only wonder what she felt having her husband collapse in her arms with that kiss being their last shared moment in this Life. Similarly, Ewa and Tomek, his parents were equally devastated by Radek's passing yet little Maya, a toddler, and Marysia, still an eighth month baby, gave them, and Aleksandra, hope for rebuilding a better future.

For Lieutenant-General Politczek, whilst he had lost a senior officer and was faced by his succession planning having been torpedoed, the reality was the loss of a close friend. Mentoring Radek as a soldier and counter-intelligence officer in developing his career had been both a pleasure and privilege. His loss to Aleksandra and the Król family was incomparable but for Poland, a brave and honourable man of his stature was irreplaceable. The President and Prime Minister had voiced as much in eulogies at his funeral.

Life does of course go on with the Polish and Lithuanian Governments finally following their counter-intelligence services longstanding advice that the entire border surrounding Kaliningrad need to be properly secured. Grzegorz was particularly pleased that this Schengen Border was going to be far more than just rolls of razor wire. The concerns were that the Kremlin would seek to replicate Lukashenko's attempts in 2021 of using illegal migrants to breach the Schengen Area's Northern Border. Such an influx of asylum seekers would simply allow Russian spies and fifth columnists to slip through undetected. Disrupting Polish and Baltic equipment shipments for Ukraine's War Effort would be the logistic targets.

In France, Peter van de Berg was cycling happily through Provence having left the Rhone Valley. A further US$ four million had arrived into his Lugano account weeks ago and he had not rushed to get home to the luxury of his home in Domaine Fleurs des Bougainvillees. He was enjoying the warmth of the sunshine after the cold of a Polish Winter. Additionally, the knowledge that his various disguises and the care not to leave detectable evidence leading the Police to his door had left him with a feeling of professional satisfaction rather than smugness – a mission accomplished. At that very moment, the grimreaper took a hand as death crept up unannounced and unexpectedly on Peter.

A young group of holidaymakers were heading along the backroads from Valbonne towards Grasse. As people do from time to time, the car was being driven far too fast for a winding and curving country road. Peter stood no chance as the Peugeot came hurtling round a bend on the wrong side of the road. In that split second before he was hurtled metres into the air before crashing into the crash barrier breaking his neck instantly his facial expression was one of total surprise. Perhaps for this assassin, who was meticulous in planning his missions being caught so unexpectedly in the wrong place at the wrong time, was for him particularly ironic.

Chapter 39

Capitaine Michel Blanchard hated those days when you had to advise a loved one of a dear one's passing. It was the worst part of his job. The Valbonne Commissariat of Police had forwarded the details of Marcel Durand's death to the Nantes Commissariat. It fallen to him accompanied by Gendarme Madeleine LaCroix to break the news to a Mrs Durand who was shown to live at the address on Marcel's identity card.

Climbing the steps to the 7th floor of the State owned apartment block, the lifts were once again out of order, the Police Officers walked along the open walkway to the relevant flat door and rang the bell. The door was opened by a woman in her mid-forties who on seeing the Police Uniforms of the French National Police half-turned calling out - 'Marcel, Police are here please come'. It only took a few minutes for the Police Officers to realise the real Marcel Durand was very much alive. He worked for Nantes City Council as a garbage collector and that together with his Identification Card, proved the man who had died in Provence was travelling on a forged document. As to 'the why and who' it became once more the Valbonne Commissariat's problem.

For a fraudulent identity case such as this, the Valbonne Commissariat by law had to notify the Bouches-du-Rhône Police Prefecture. The Prefecture had responsibility for serious crime and counter-terrorism. A young detective, Monique Vicot, looked through the contents of the fake Marcel Durand. A cycling map from Besancon to the South of France with various hostels marked and some eight thousand euros in cash made her question why, unless a very keen cyclist was this man who also had a Deutsche bank card in the name of Dieter Müller roughing it seemingly in hostels rather than two or three star hotels or better. When, with the help of colleagues in Germany's Federal Police (Bundespolizei), she discovered Mr Müller had nearly three hundred thousand euros in the account, security concerns and thresholds became heightened within the Bouches-du-Rhône Police Prefecture. The decision was taken to circulate across television media and newspapers a picture of Peter asking members of the French Public to contact them. The man had died in a tragic road accident whilst cycling along the Grasse to Valbonne road. Without any identification documents on his person, the Police were unable to contact his nearest and dearest with the sad news. A designated telephone line was established with calls transferred automatically to Detective Vicot's number.

There were the expected calls in the following days from the various hostels where Dieter Müller had stayed together with a number of his cycling companions phoning in also confirming his name was Marcel Durand. When questioned no one professed to have ever heard of a Dieter Müller and with that surname being the most common across Germany, the Bundespolizei had indicated, having followed up on the address in Deutsche Bank's records, which turned out to be a cleared building site, there were not the resources to do more at this time. Feeling somewhat despondent, Monique picked up the phone. It was the tearful housekeeper of a Peter van de Berg who lived in Domaine Fleurs des Bougainvillees.

Chapter 40

Grzegorz's Friday meeting had commenced with him introducing Matt Elliott, on secondment from the British Ministry of Defence and MI6, who would be temporarily taking over the duties previously dealt with by Radek. Matt was of course well known to Jan and Witoria even prior to Radek's military funeral at the GROM's Gdansk Garrison and Headquarters. They had all worked together with Radek in 2018 exposing the GRU's embedded spies across Europe and also the Ukrainian Mafia's criminal empire. Grzegorz's efforts to entice retired Colonel Kuba Pawlukowicz back to ABW until a suitable permanent appointment could be made had failed. Hence with the UK and Polish Ministries of Defence working ever more closely in supporting Ukraine's war effort, the offer of a well-qualified and battle proven MI6 officer as a temporary secondee was grasped with welcoming hands by Grzegorz.

The handset on Grzegorz's desk began to ring incessantly and a reluctant Grzegorz left the conference table. Why on earth would Major Pawel Adamski, his aide de camp, need to interrupt his weekly meeting? Was it the President, Prime Minister, or another Cabinet Member? Having picked up the phone, he listened intently – 'OK Pawel put him through.' Turning towards Jan, Witoria, and Matt seated around the conference, he spoke 'Inspektor Landa … I am with my senior colleagues … I am putting you on loudspeaker.'

'Good morning General and to your colleagues, I have good and bad news regarding Colonel Krol's assassin. With full credit to the detectives of the Bouches-du-Rhône Police Prefecture, it is now beyond doubt that a Dutch national, Peter van de Berg was his murderer and, subject to further on-going investigations, is more than probably the assassin known in the criminal underworld and dark net as the Surgeon. Sadly, the man is dead so Poland and the Król Family will not have the closure that a trial before the Polish Courts would bring. Perhaps on reflection much of such a trial would have been held 'in camera' given the sensitivity of ABW's counter-intelligence work; let alone the motive for the assassination highlighting embarrassingly Poland's direct involvement in Ukraine's War across the Forests of Sumy last Spring in the early days of Russia's 2nd invasion. Peter van de Berg was a master of disguise with exemplary attention to detail. If he had not been killed in a road accident and the detective work of the French National Police and DGSE Counter-Intelligence, I doubt if we would have ever got to the bottom of Radek Król's murder. A full report covering Van de Berg's arrival in Niepolomice leading up to the assassination, his subsequent escape as far as Besancon, and then to the South of France is now being compiled. With regard to progress by the French Authorities following full access to his large property in Domaine Fleurs des Bougainvillees, details of their initial investigations point to his involvement in many unsolved murders so the truth will eventually come out in respect of these earlier crimes. However, such an investigation will undoubtedly take some months, which will include seizure of his assets and charging of any accomplices.'

'Thank you Inspektor. Have the President and Prime Minister been informed?'

'Yes General.'

THE END

Many thanks for reading 'Reprisal'. If you enjoyed the story, and have a moment to spare, then I would really appreciate a short review on the novel being left at your purchasing store or favourite stores' websites. Your help in spreading the word is gratefully received

NOVELS BY JOE DANIEL

CONDUCT BECOMING as an ebook in January 2020-
link if UK www.amazon.co.uk/dp/B083P5KW9C
link if Poland or worldwide
www.amazon.com/dp/B083P5KW9C

CONDUCT BECOMING*as a paperback in July 2020-
link if UK www.amazon.co.uk/dp/B08D54RGCW
link if Poland or worldwide
www.amazon.com/dp/B08D54RGCW

SOFIA'S LAW as an ebook in June 2020-
link if UK www.amazon.co.uk/dp/B08B44P89G
link if Poland or worldwide
www.amazon.com/dp/B08B44P89G

SOFIA'S LAW*as a paperback in July 2020-
link if UK www.amazon.co.uk/dp/B08BWHQ9D4
link if Poland or worldwide
www.amazon.com/dp/B08BWHQ9D4

BRAMSTON GREEN as an ebook in November 2020-
link if UK www.amazon.co.uk/dp/B08MCB33JT
link if Poland or worldwide
www.amazon.com/dp/B08MCB33JT

BRAMSTON GREEN* as a paperback in November 2020-
link if UK www.amazon.co.uk/dp/B08M8CRLT6
link if Poland or worldwide
www.amazon.com/dp/B08M8CRLT6

THAT'S LIFE as an ebook in August 2021-
link if UK www.amazon.co.uk/dp/B09DX36VN5
link if Poland or worldwide
www.amazon.com/dp/B09DX36VN5

THAT'S LIFE* as a paperback in August 2021-
link if UK www.amazon.co.uk/dp/B09DMTVKR3
link if Poland or worldwide
www.amazon.com/dp/B09DMTVKR3

RUSSIAN STRATAGEM as an ebook in June 2022-
link if UK www.amazon.co.uk/dp/B0B4Y6WGG6
link if Poland or worldwide
www.amazon.com/dp/B0B4Y6WGG6

RUSSIAN STRATAGEM* as a paperback in June 2022-
link if UK www.amazon.co.uk/dp/B0B4K1BWNX
link if Poland or worldwide
www.amazon.com/dp/B0B4K1BWNX

REPRISAL as an ebook in May 2023-
link if UK www.amazon.co.uk/dp/B0C62BJPDB
link if Poland or worldwide
www.amazon.com/dp/B0C62BJPDB

REPRISAL* as a paperback in May 2023-
link if UK www.amazon.co.uk/dp/B0C6BFB789

link if Poland or worldwide
www.amazon.com/dp/B0C6BFB789

*[*all the titles were planned for conversion into Audio Books utilising the services of ACX by Audible.com, an Amazon.com subsidiary, and a leading provider of audio content and entertainment. Release had been planned for 2023. However, a combination of COVID in California and technical issues have temporarily delayed this still positive intention]*

Printed in Great Britain
by Amazon